ageing disgracefully

ageing disgracefully

Short Stories about Disreputable Old People

COLIN COTTERILL

Heaven Lake Press

Distributed by:
Asia Document Bureau Ltd.
P.O. Box 1029
Nana Post Office
Bangkok 10112 Thailand
Fax: (662) 260-4578
Web site: http://www.heavenlakepress.com
email: editorial@heavenlakepress.com

Heaven Lake Press paperback edition 2010

ISBN 978-616-90393-5-8

44

Contents

Gran Larceny ⋗⋗⋗ 1

A Night on the Tiles ⋗⋗⋗ 27

Jack Wong Has a Rare Moment of Lucidity ⋗⋗⋗ 38

Tart ⋗⋗⋗ 46

The One Legged Marathon Runner of 12B
     Wildebeest Crescent ⋗⋗⋗ 63

The Inside Job ⋗⋗⋗ 85

Has Anyone Seen Mrs. Lightswitch? ⋗⋗⋗ 101

Fanta Man ⋗⋗⋗ 124

Playing Grand Theft Auto III With Death ⋗⋗⋗ 148

It's a Dog s Life (In Four Short Acts) ⋗⋗⋗ 164

Ode to a Siam Square Pizza ⋗⋗⋗ 166

Life as a Torreja ⋗⋗⋗ 191

Collecting Old Footprints ⋗⋗⋗ 222

A Slightly Embellished True Story from the Gulf
     of Siam ⋗⋗⋗ 242

Coconuts ⋗⋗⋗ 249

Forked ⋗⋗⋗ 273

Hello

...and welcome to my first short story/graphic collection: Ageing Disgracefully. All the stories but one look at the lives of people who have passed the middle age of sixty and are, or have been, behaving badly.

We travel, through these stories, from England, where I was born, to Southeast Asia, where I live. On the journey we visit Australia and the U.S of A, and we learn that disgusting old people can be found just about anywhere.

In the stories you'll meet people you recognize as well as one or two traits and wiles that you'll probably recognize in yourself. This book is a confirmation that life 'begins, rather than ends in decade number seven.

We visit the troubled minds of murderers, bank robbers, practical jokers, serial killers, perverts and just plain liars, all of whom are old enough to know better. Where I thought words would be insufficient to adequately describe the pure awfulness, I have resorted to pictures.

I have had a marvelous time putting this collection together and sharing its stories with friends. I hope you enjoy it every bit as much.

Best Wishes

Colin Cotterill

Gran Larceny

IT ALL STARTED as a lesson. Well, no, not a lesson exactly, more an example. The type of example you think will have one effect and it turns out to have an entirely different one. In Hilda's case it was a life-altering example that partly explained why on this October 2nd she was holed up in the New Malden branch of Safeway with an HK G36 carbine and thirty-eight hostages. Hilda had been a home-help with the Borough Council for forty years which was hardly appropriate background training for hostage negotiation. Ten minutes earlier, a mobile telephone had arrived at the supermarket door on the back of a small remote-controlled robot. A check-out girl had gone to fetch it. Hilda had been yes and no'ing into it for an inordinately long time. She looked up and called out to the captivated customers. "So I'm using a crutch, what's it to you?" asked Patten in the face of a low-life squinting over a bottle of Singha Gold.

"She wants to know if any of you have special needs."

There was a moment of surprised silence before one anemic-looking teenager raised his arm. In his fist was a plastic bag that had been clenched there since the automatic weapon fire smashed the florescent light above his head. Small glass nicks dappled his cheeks.

"I've got dyslexia," he said.

Forgetting she was holding the gun, Hilda swung around to look at him. Considering it can dispense seven hundred and fifty rounds a minute, the HK G36 is an impressively light weapon. It's easy to think you're holding an umbrella. The hostages, all but one old dear with knee replacements (who had been provided a chair), were sitting on the ground. As the muzzle swung in their direction they threw themselves flat on the floor and screamed. Hilda observed the fracas with a look of shock on her face.

"Oh, dear," she said. "I'm sorry. I didn't mean ..."

The words jammed in her throat. She wanted to cry. What an absolute bloody mess. She wanted to throw off her stocking mask, drop to her knees and sob. But instead she stood perfectly still and felt her chin bob up and down of its own accord. The hostages interpreted her bout of depression—the squeezed expression beneath the mask—as a manic moment, a dip into derangement. They knew from countless TV thrillers and novels that it was at times such as these that something clicks in the killer's mind and thirty-eight innocent victims are mowed down, an ornamental fountain of blood. Nothing in the frozen goods section was more rigid at that second than the shoppers inside the eerily quiet Safeway.

To ease the tension, and prevent herself from having a personal urinary accident, the large Jamaican floor manageress took it upon herself to speak. She turned to the boy and said, "I don't think that's what she means, love. I think she's talking about food, allergies and diet and all that. Am I right, dear?"

Hilda didn't respond so a grumpy old fellow dressed in crumpled Oxfam cast offs asked, "Is it? Is that what you mean?"

Hilda seemed to arrive back in Safeway like a Star Trek transporter beam passenger. She looked around to get her bearings.

"What?" she asked. "Oh, yes. Yes. Food." She placed the gun carefully beside the cash register—barrel facing the street—and sat back in the cashier's seat.

"They're preparing food?" said the grumpy man, buoyed by the fact she'd put down her weapon. Without it she looked like nothing more than an elderly lady with a thick tan stocking over her head.

"Yes."

"What for?"

"What?"

"Why are they preparing us food? We're in a bleeding supermarket. We could survive here for a year. Don't you think it's a bit suspicious?"

"It's a trick," said the dyslexic. "They detonate a stun-bomb in a sandwich box and the SAS rush us while we're all off our heads."

"Will you two shut up?" came a muffled male voice from the gallery. One poor soul had obviously been hoping for a Special Forces raid to end the siege. Hilda looked down at her lap and nodded.

"You're right," she said.

She looked at her left hand. A voice like that of a tiny trapped person was calling from the cell-phone.

"Are you there? Are you there?"

Hilda raised the phone to her ear.

"Yes," she said. "No. Be quiet and listen. We won't be needing catering . . . Because this is a bleeding supermarket, that's why. Do you think we're completely stupid?"

There was a barely perceivable hint of a smile beneath the stocking. Her choice of pronoun clearly confused some of the hostages who looked around for an accomplice, a second shooter. Hilda would have slammed the phone shut at that moment to emphasize her thus-far unconvincing dominance of the situation, but it was a clever device devoid of an off button. The channel was permanently open. But for the tub of coleslaw she would have had to listen to the whiny insect voice incessantly.

She was ten yards from the cash register packing diced cabbage and carrots around the mobile when she remembered the gun. She turned to see one bold shelf-stacking boy on his feet and closer to the cash register than her. He was as lanky as a greyhound on a rack.

If she'd charged for the gun there was no doubt she would have lost the race. Instead, she surprised herself by setting her haunches back on the disabled dairy cooler and reaching inside her topcoat. And there, in their respective positions, they froze, the boy five yards from a loaded weapon, Hilda Broadstock with her hand on her bus pass.

She didn't look much like the woman in the photograph on that bus pass today. She didn't have much in common with her either. Five months earlier that woman had walked into the Tooting High Street branch of the HSBC bank, stood in a queue and made a rash decision. And the same day that woman had vanished in a puff of smoke and Hilda II had risen from her ashes. And all because of one teller whose mother had forgotten to tell her, "Just because you're having a bad day, doesn't mean you have to make everyone else miserable." Ten customers and one teller on duty. Perhaps the other staff were off sick. Perhaps the bank was on the brink of financial collapse and one teller was all they could afford. But, for whatever reason, there was one teller and she wasn't having the best of days. She snapped at some little woman who'd signed the wrong box of the withdrawal form. She made a sarcastic comment when someone asked if they could make a transfer into an account at a different bank.

Hilda watched all this from the queue, feeling like part of a conveyor of sausage meat about to be snapped off and tied at the ends. There were grumbled comments fore and aft.

"Someone's had a bit of a barney with someone's boyfriend, if you ask me."

"Her ladyship didn't get her Weetabix this morning."

"She must be foreign."

But Hilda wasn't about to give her the benefit of any doubts. She put the girl's bad manners down to genes. She could tell from her stuck up accent she thought she was better than everyone else. Hilda had been working with toffee-nosed, so-called high-class old bags for forty years. She'd brought them tea and scrubbed their toilets and been treated like a door mat for her efforts. One skinny old crow called Edna had thought she was her daughter and blamed her for stealing the family jewels. Bill had reached for her tits at the slightest excuse. Mildred spat a lot. There had been hundreds over the years. Most of them disliked Hilda as much as she disliked them.

The ones that pretended to be nice to her were the ex-nuns or retired voluntary workers from leper colonies in Africa. They talked to her as if she were one of the underfed illiterates in the third world. She could imagine them at the cribbage tables: "Oh, yes. I talk to my servant. We have a warm relationship."

Oh, really? If it was that warm, why didn't they hand over some of that unused cash stashed under the floorboards? Rich as Christmas cake some of those old biddies and they gave her fifty pence as a New Year bonus. You could buy yourself a nice stick of licorice for that. They'd told her at the council to show respect to the old folks, but forcing herself to be pleasant for forty years had taken a lot out of Hilda. When Mr. Broadstock was still alive her income helped pay for those little luxuries. The week in Littlehampton. New curtains for the living room. And back in those days she knew that if any of her old people got out of line she could always tell them to go take a long run off a short pier. She didn't need the job, she'd tell them. She could walk out anytime.

But the tobacco fairies had taken Mr. Broadstock unexpectedly before his fortieth and Hilda was left alone with only a small insurance handout, and her cleaning salary. She had no education to speak of and no skills. She couldn't tell anyone to jump off anything. She had no choice but to put up with them. Some were demented, others were just rude. This bank girl was forty years their junior but she was from the same stock. Hilda knew the lass would be making people's lives a misery when she was sixty. She'd decided then and there to make an example of her. As the queue inched forward she took out an old envelope and ripped off the back. She fished around in her handbag for a biro and wrote a short note.

'Ok, bitch. I've got a gun and its pointed at your ugly face. Give me all the money from the draw or I'll blow your head off.' For good measure she added. *'I'm serius.'*

She contemplated using the "f" word, but she'd never been that fond of it and decided the message was threatening enough without it. She was astounded at how good it felt to have that note in her hand.

What she had in mind was to show the girl the message, wait for her to pee her pants, then give her a piece of her mind. That was the plan if you could call it such. No less than she deserved. Perhaps a woman who loved her job and her life wouldn't have handed over that note. Another woman might have been more concerned about consequences. But Hilda had gone to the bank that afternoon to cash her long-service bonus cheque on the ultimate day of her employment. They'd had a party for her. Two slices of Madeira cake wrapped in tin foil were squashed at the bottom of her shopping bag under the greengrocery. The flush from three glasses of sherry still stained her cheeks. In her speech the district manager had called her Helen and nobody corrected him. So Hilda wasn't really of a mind to consider consequences.

Having read the note, the teller asked calmly, "Is this a hoax?"

Hilda didn't answer. She glared. She had an impressive glare. She'd practiced it often behind the backs of her charges. But it concerned her greatly that the girl wasn't thrown into a panic. Hilda reached into her bag and took hold of a cucumber. She pushed it against the fabric of the bag until it produced a small bulge. She drew the teller's attention to it with her eyebrows and allowed herself to imagine that it really was a gun, that she could actually blow the girl's head off. And it was probably the menace of that thought which crossed her brow and caused the teller a moment of doubt.

What happened next had rather surprised Hilda. The girl had calmly collected all the bank notes from the tray and stacked them neatly on the counter in front of her. Hilda stared at them. The teller made no apparent moves towards an alarm button. She sat with a bored expression on her face as if she'd been robbed most of the days of her life. Hilda felt like she was floating, drifting from the universe. She had fallen into, if not a black hole, then, at least, a dark mauve one. She saw herself scoop the money into her bag, pull down the rim of her lilac sun bonnet and head to the door. She expected it to be sealed, but with a little push it gave way and she was street-bound and free.

The lanky shelf-stacker was starting to wobble. It had been a mistake to stop mid-stride. He'd had his chance and it had passed him by.

"Go on, get it," said the same man who'd hoped for an SAS rescue.

"Go on, get it," Hilda urged. "I dare you." Her hand was still inside the lapel of her coat.

"She's bluffing," said the man.

Hilda's smile spread like a run in the stocking.

"Daren, come and sit down," said the manageress. "The lady probably doesn't want any more trouble than she's already got."

Daren seemed delighted to have the pressure off him and gladly returned to his place on the cool tiles. Hilda returned to the cashier's seat and plonked herself down as if her weight had tripled over the past hour.

If only she'd had the common sense to quit while she was ahead. But the adrenalin had sped through her veins like a fast-acting energy drink. She could have taken her two thousand, two hundred and thirty-eight pounds and considered herself very fortunate. But she hadn't exhibited any common sense. Not a shred. She'd gone to the White Hart on the night of the heist to calm her nerves. She was in an alcove with a double G&T and she overheard the conversation of two sweaty geezers at the bar. Her DARING DAYLIGHT ROBBERY was on page two of the *Evening Standard* and they were voicing their opinions of it.

"Says she was an old fart. Seventy at least. The cameras didn't pick up 'er face cause of 'er 'at."

"Good luck to 'er."

"Good luck? Since when 'ave you been a fan of armed robbery?"

"You don't know she was armed."

"Teller says she 'ad a sawed off shotgun."

"Ridiculous. Why risk a weapon charge when you can just waltz in to any bank and give 'em a fretening note and they'll 'and over the cash no questions asked?"

"You're barmy."

"It's the policy. I saw it on the news. All the bank staff are told if there's a likeli'ood of bodily 'arm—just a chance—they shouldn't make a fuss. Just 'and over the money and button their lips. Leave it up to the cops to sort out."

Hilda had thought long and hard about that comment as she lay sleepless on her mattress that night. She was still feeding off the excitement from the heist, astounded at how easy it had been. From HSBC she'd walked calmly to the tube station, smiled at the coloured boy at the wicket, and traveled unaccompanied by the sound of pursuing sirens to South Wimbledon. Her blood had buzzed the whole time. And now there was a suggestion that she could do it again, that she could re-experience the high and might not even have need of a cucumber.

The second robbery had been more stressful, of course. The anticipation had lain heavy in her gut like a sack of salt. She'd put on an old pair of Mr. B's thick-lens glasses that made her look like an ornamental fish staring out of a bowl. Her hair was hidden beneath a large Paisley scarf as favoured by Her Majesty. There had been no queue and she had no personal grievance against the teller. He was a middleaged man with shaving wounds and a bad-hair life. He'd smiled at Hilda and wished her a good morning. She'd handed him her note. The vacuum cleaner attachment poked from the raincoat she carried over her arm. She had contemplated coming unarmed but at the last minute had felt a need for the security of a weapon.

And it happened again exactly as it had done in Tooting. Despite the fact that the vacuum cleaner attachment looked suspiciously like a vacuum cleaner attachment the teller emptied the drawer and placed the banknotes on the counter. He seemed to be struggling for a bank platitude to bid her on her way, but the manual obviously hadn't included a scenario for armed robbery. Instead, he raised his palms to show that was all he had and managed a half smile.

Thus, Hilda's life of crime had begun. A different disguise for each bank, a new frock, a wig, dark glasses, Mr. B's old false teeth. It wasn't that she looked remarkably different each time. The same woman appeared in each of the CCTV stills they published in the newspapers. But, the important fact was that she looked like a million other women her age. She had no distinguishing features other than the disguise she'd chosen for the day. She supposed it was the same for Superman. Put a pair of glasses on him and you wouldn't know him from an office clerk. Not even her neighbours gave a thought that it might be Hilda they saw in the photographs. The tabloids christened her GRAN LARCENY, but despite her fame none of the tellers recognized her until after she'd handed them her notes. They'd all been expecting a star. Celebrities were invariably disappointing in real life. This old lady hobbling into the bank on swollen ankles couldn't possibly be . . .

Rather than let the hostages loose to forage for themselves, Hilda sent the Safeway staff off to gather food and drink for everyone. Someone went to the pharmacy aisle and brought back tweezers, plasters and Germoline to treat the wounded. Hilda hadn't intended to hurt anyone. The gun had just gone off. She'd been appalled at how sensitive it was, police issue and all. No wonder innocent bystanders were hit so often. She considered writing to her member of parliament about it. She'd merely lofted it above her head so everyone could see it and the trigger had virtually pulled itself. Hilda must have hit every florescent light in the building. For a few seconds the supermarket had been the scene of a Nordic ice storm. She'd thought how nice it would have looked in slow motion.

In real time it had been chaotic; screaming people running into stacks of Brillo Pads, throwing themselves beneath the fruit and vegetable bins. Passersby in the street pointing and shouting that someone should do something. The long-necked driver of a car running into a lamppost. Hilda standing in the entrance with the automatic glass doors opening and closing behind her like slowly clapping hands. It was out of concern that the panicking shoppers might injure themselves more so than a demonstration of power that she told them all to freeze where they were. Being slaughtered in a public area had become commonplace in 21st Century society so all twenty-nine shoppers and nine staff had allowed themselves to be herded like cattle to the dairy section.

The florescent wounds were all superficial but would certainly look impressive on the evening news. And there seemed to be a subdued but palpable air of sinful pleasure as everyone tucked into their pillaged supermarket feasts. Someone had the bright idea of taking all the beer cans out of the cooler to wash down the meal. Even non-drinkers were enjoying their lagers with thoughts of 'the condemned man ate a hearty meal' passing through their minds.

"You want one, love?" the manageress asked. She was holding a ham roll in her right hand and a London Pride in her right.

"Yeah, why not?" Hilda decided.

The Safeway lady was twice Hilda's size and looked as if she could bench-press a stacked pallet of canned tuna. It wouldn't have been that difficult for her to subdue the little woman in the stocking mask and wrest the gun from her, but she merely handed over the lunch and smiled.

"I have days like this," she said.

In spite of everything, Hilda laughed.

"Is that so? You mean days when you rob a bank, steal a gun and hold a shop full of people hostage?"

"Yeah, well, I mean, not quite as horrible as that, but it's the same principle. Everything goes wrong from the moment you wake up and whatever you do to try to make it better just seems to make it all worse. Tell me I'm not right."

"No. You've summed it up very nicely," Hilda agreed.

Perhaps Hilda had become a little overconfident. She'd singled out a branch of Barclays in New Malden. The plan was that she'd use her bus pass to get there on the number 131 then come home on the South West Trains line via Raynes Park. She'd even picked out a screening at the Odeon that she planned to attend after the robbery. Everything was sorted out. She'd cased the joint the previous day to see how long it would take her to get to the station.

As far as the day's outfit went, Hilda had decided to go with a burgundy topcoat with a peacock broach above the left breast, and a heavy-duty tan stocking as a mask. It was a decision she had come to rue long before she confronted the teller with her note. This was the first time she'd attempted a disguise that needed donning before a robbery. Previously, she had worn her accessories to the bank and discarded them in a rubbish receptacle during her escape. But she had been rather taken by the cinema images of desperate criminals, their faces distorted into a mean grimace by a common stocking. She had tried several from her bottom drawer before arriving at the HD tan. It made her look particularly ferocious and somewhat Indian. But it had been necessary to stop in the doorway of the bank to put it on. And that's where the troubles had begun. As she was pulling it over her head, a greasy-haired bank customer on her way out had noticed her beside the door.

She'd stopped and stared at Hilda who wished her a good morning and told the woman the stocking was a little tight. She was having trouble getting it over her earrings. She had probably expected the witness to come forward after the robbery rather than go directly to the New Malden police station, which is in fact what she'd done. So by the time the teller had emptied her tray and Hilda was on her way out of the bank, a recently-polished police car was already parked in front with three officers crouched behind it. They had obviously been influenced by American cop shows as five years earlier the police would have strolled calmly into the bank and said, "You're nicked, lady." A friendly wander to the police station and the case closed.

Now the police were obliged to assume you had explosives taped to your corset. According to the Homeland Security guidelines they had to set up a siege scenario and call in a SWAT team, and a situation that could have been resolved calmly and in good humour would be turned into a panic fest. This is exactly what had happened. Hilda's weapon of the day was an old lead tap she'd found in Mr. B's tool chest. From a distance it looked like a handgun and, when Hilda lofted it to show the teller there was nothing to be afraid about, there came frenzied shouts from the street and the shiny police car was removed to the far side of the road. Traffic was halted and a cordon was stretched across the street to keep back gawkers and violence addicts.

Hilda had looked at the teller and said, "Oh, bugger."

The teller, Stephanie, a young thing who had erstwhile considered bank work to be dull and monotonous, smiled at her robber. "You're Gran Larceny, aren't you?"

"I'm up shit creek without a paddle is what I am," Hilda replied.

"Can I have your autograph?"

For want of a better plan, Hilda had signed a withdrawal form and made the dedication out to '*My darling, Steve*', but by then there was an awful lot of activity in front of the bank. Hilda could see actual weapons that had never once been connected to a sink, people in flack jackets running between doorways, the backs of a number of television live-at-the-scene reporters. She helped herself to one of Stephanie's extra strong peppermints and pondered.

"You're in a tricky spot," Stephanie had told her.

Hilda hadn't been about to refute that observation, bloody obvious as it was.

"I don't suppose you've got a secret escape route?" Hilda asked.

"There's the back door."

Hilda considered the odds. Several hundred people out in the street, weapons trained on the bank from every rooftop, and nobody guarding the back door? She didn't have great faith in the English police force but even they wouldn't be that stupid.

". . . and the side door," Stephanie continued.

"What's a side door?"

"It goes through to the bakery. This block all used to be connected before the bank moved in. They call it a fire escape but we use it to get warm doughnuts fresh from the oven."

As per the protocol, the bakery and twenty businesses on either side of the bank had been evacuated. Hilda had paused briefly to sample a Bakewell tart on her way through to the rear of the establishment. She'd figured if she was going to be peppered with machine gun fire, at least she would have tasted a little piece of heaven before heading off down to hell. She opened the back door expecting to be confronted by an army of police, but all she saw was an HK G36 carbine leaning against the garden wall. Of course she didn't know what it was called. It was just a big gun to Hilda. To her right she saw the back of a black-clad police-man urinating into the raspberry bushes. It occurred to her for the first time that even SWAT personnel on a siege needed to relieve themselves. Nervous tension quickly found its way to the bladder and there had been no time to bring in Porta-loos.

Hilda had left the door ajar, collected the weapon, and crept out through the back gate. She'd found herself in an alleyway just a few steps behind two gentlemen in plain clothes who were seated at a small bank of monitors on the back of a van. On the screens were views of the bank from the outside, front and rear, as well as two internal bank CCTV feeds. The police had been watching her activities inside the bank but obviously hadn't yet learned of the side door. Luck was playing center forward on Hilda's team. The men were wired up to microphones and too engrossed in their monitoring to bother with movement behind them. Hilda headed down the alleyway in the opposite direction trying to keep her wobbly legs from giving out beneath her. Flight was the only thing on her mind. She was on the verge of discarding the gun and the stocking mask by chucking them over somebody's garden fence, but two things happened to belay that thought.

As she reached the end of the alleyway a voice from behind her called out, "Oy, that's my gun. Shit, it's her."

At the same time, two women officers barely out of their teens by the looks of them passed by the mouth of the alleyway and turned their heads to see Hilda coming at them with a shopping bag in one hand and a loaded carbine in the other. Hilda hoisted the weapon. The jaws of the police girls dropped in unison.

"Nobody needs to get hurt," Hilda said. There was always room for a healthy cliché in stressful situations.

Hilda wasn't wearing her sensible shoes. The only pair she had that didn't clash with the burgundy topcoat had two-inch heels and pinched a little. She'd started to take note of the witness descriptions of her attire and she didn't want to look like a slob in the eyes of *Daily Mirror* readers. But, the point was, she hadn't been about to do any running in two-inch heels. She told the girls to put up their hands and walk away from her. As they did so, Hilda started off along New Malden High Street. Although there were no cars, there were several people who had tired of nothing happening at the police cordon and were going about their business. Their reaction to an elderly lady with a stocking over her head and a large gun had been peculiar. Nobody screamed or fled. There was a possibility she was with the police, but then again ... there wasn't. Mothers from New Malden's large Korean community shepherded their children away from Hilda and two young thugs gave her a peace sign.

She had just been passing Safeway when the policeman reached the end of the alley and called out, "You! Stop!" Pedestrians turned to look at him, then at Hilda, and that was when she'd decided to duck inside the supermarket.

The negotiator was using a bullhorn from across the street. It made her sound like a frog. Hilda wasn't paying any attention. She was sitting on a stool opposite the manageress telling her the entire story. The hostages were still sitting on the floor but the gathering was looking less like a primary school hymn service and more like Woodstock. Empty cartons and beer cans littered the floor around them. Two hostages had asked permission to go to the toilet and both had returned to resume their drinking. The dyslexic was having as much trouble with his speaking as with his reading. The Oxfam man had removed his shoes and a noticeable bad-sock gap was opening between him and the others. Word had made the rounds that they were being held hostage by Gran Larceny which made this something of a celebrity event. As hostage situations went it was a very jolly affair. But there was always the danger of the police storming the building and accidentally shooting everyone. That might have been at the back of the manageress's mind when she made her suggestion.

It was 3 p.m. The New Malden Safeway standoff had been ongoing for five hours. The news reporters were running short of things to say. They'd fallen back on the weather. There had been no demands from the hostage-taker and no obvious signs of aggression. The supermarket CCTV had been disconnected in-store so the police were planning their assault-raid blind. There was a high likelihood of casualties. The hostage negotiator had lost her voice and was sipping a hot lemon juice. She was surprised to hear the mobile telephone on the table in front of her crackle into life.

"Hello," she croaked.

"Don't talk. Just listen," came a voice. "I'm releasing the women. Try not to shoot them. You'll see they're all unarmed."

Before the woman had a chance to reply, the supermarket doors opened and a large throng of females edged forward with their hands in the air. The negotiator heard a low whistle from one of the male officers. The hostages walked slowly onto the pavement. Some were giggling. It was a wonder they didn't all freeze to death because they were wearing nothing but bras, panties and shoes. They walked to the kerb huddled together like a flock of ducks, some pushing and barging, some making comments like, "Bugger me, it's cold." A police sergeant behind the squad car beckoned them forward.

"I've got a shot at Gran," came a voice over the chief inspector's headphones that hung loosely around his neck. He looked up to see the woman they'd all been referring to as Gran standing back in the shadows of the doorway watching the women flee to safety. She was holding the stolen weapon against her chest. One of the snipers opposite had a clear view of her in her sights. The chief inspector only had a few seconds to consider all the ramifications and make the call. But it was clearly laid out in the anti-terror handbook that a criminal brandishing a weapon was a threat to the public and an appropriate target. This opportunity might not occur again and he'd live to rue his lack of decisiveness if he kept quiet now.

"Take the shot," he said.

The sniper fired twice and the 'snap, snap' of her rifle sent the women in the street into a wild panic. There were screams. They ran, young, old, small, extra-large into the arms of the waiting police who noticed a strong odour of beer fumes on their breaths.

"Target is down," came the sniper's voice.

"Well done, lass," said the chief inspector. He called for his men to move forward with caution. As they were crossing the road, the male hostages began to drift out through the open doors. It was a scene reminiscent of closing time at the pub. They were clearly drunk. Some were singing, "I shot the sheriff." Others were holding each other up, arms locked together. The police were confused. They looked back at the CI for guidance.

"Just confirm the old woman's down and get her gun before one of those clowns picks it up," he called to them.

He stood in the middle of the street like a gunslinger while his people ran crouching, combat-style, into the supermarket. He was keen to be in there with them but the protocol didn't allow it. From deep inside he heard faint, "Aisle two, clear. Aisle five, clear. Bathrooms clear." This continued until all the aisles and back rooms were accounted for. At last the police emerged from the supermarket with their weapons lowered and their helmets in their hands. The senior officer saluted his superior.

"No sign of her, Chief," he said. "But we did find this."

Two officers were stretchering what, from a distance, appeared to be the victim of a steamroller accident. On closer inspection it turned out to be a life-sized advertising cutout of Leona Lewis, who had been a popular winner of Britain's X-Factor in 2006 and had sold her soul to a baked beans manufacturer. Her cutout stood seductively in every Safeway in the country. But elsewhere she was probably not dressed in a burgundy top coat or wearing a stocking over her head. She certainly wouldn't have been holding an HK G36 carbine, nor would she have sported two neat bullet holes through her chest.

The chief inspector kicked at an imagined football and clicked open his chest mike.

"Don't let any of those women get away," he shouted. "Grab every last one of them."

Deep in his heart he probably knew it was too late even then. He walked rather than run back to the department store where the hostages were being re-briefed and debriefed. His lack of urgency was perhaps indicative of the loss of hope he held of catching his perpetrator. He did have a chance to interview all the staff and customers. Nobody seemed to have noticed when Gran Larceny and Leona Lewis changed places. None of the women were aware of the presence of one hostage who hadn't been with them during the beer binge. The instruction for the women to strip and walk out had been passed on by the manageress but the latter had obviously been in fear of her life. Nobody could fault her. Some of the female police officers on duty in the store vaguely recalled a nondescript elderly lady amongst the hostages. There was a suggestion she'd helped herself to a duffle coat from the display cabinet and headed for the public restrooms. That was the last anyone had seen of her.

And it was the last anyone heard of Gran Larceny. The tabloids moved along to other trivial pursuits and Hilda Broadstock returned to being a quiet but more complete retiree. For five months she had been the darling of the media. She'd ridden her luck but had amassed a comfortable nest egg along the way. She had avoided being shot and had not found it necessary to kill or violate anyone else. She was voted MOST POPULAR VILLAIN OF THE YEAR by *Crime Spree Quarterly*. She was the people's bank robber who stole on behalf of everyone who had the desire but not the backbone to do so themselves. Although there followed a spate of copycat robberies over the following months, none of the thieves attracted the same attention or received the same affection as Gran.

Her final act of daring had been to open a bank account in the New Malden branch of Barclays. Stephanie helped her with the paperwork and had no idea who she was dealing with. Hilda bought a Bakewell tart in the cake shop and strolled into Safeway on her way home. The manageress was stacking dog food. Her official Safeway jacket was over the back of the step ladder. Hilda slipped an envelope containing two thousand pounds into the pocket without being seen then she turned and left. She was only too aware that you couldn't buy kindness, but you could certainly invest in it.

Gran Larceny.

Until her retirement, my mum worked for the borough council as a home-help for old folk around Wimbledon. By the end, she wasn't much younger than the people she took care of. But she's a Duracell bunny, is my mum. She's 83 now and she's out dancing every Saturday night with her gentle-man friend.

But I didn't base Hilda on my mum. The latter enjoys a bit of hard work and she didn't have too hard a time with the oldies. Yet she'd be the first to tell you there were one or two buggers amongst them. And my mum isn't shy about speaking her mind. I doubt she would have held up a bank but she would certainly have given that rude teller a piece of her mind.

Mum lives in New Malden now, affectionately known as little Seoul. I'm amazed so many Koreans would travel half way around the world to settle somewhere so... dull. The Safeways hostage drama was the only exciting thing that's ever happened there... and I made it up.

POETIC LICENSE

No: 328282

COLIN COTTERILL
PO BOX 1.
NORTH OF KATMANDU

D.O.B
2.10.82

I apologize to the New Malden Chamber of Commerce for rearranging their shops and banks. I have a poetic license.

A Night on the Tiles

THERE WERE TWO distinct sounds amidst the otherwise eerie silence of the Toorak bungalow that night. One was the hiss of the cistern refilling and refilling. Edna prayed for it to stop but she knew that unless somebody pressed the lever, held it down, then released it quickly with a sort of wrist flick it would go on hissing and refilling all night. It was one of those mechanical devices that took on moody human characteristics in old age. She hoped that the man didn't have the imagination to equate the noise with the fact there might be someone actually on the toilet. She'd been using the pronoun 'he' in her mind because as a girl at the beginning of the last century she'd been raised with the belief that only men committed acts of violence and vandalism. She smiled despite the pain and followed her mind into her past.

Her second husband, Robert was there waiting for her. He'd been something of a fiend for home security. He had wires all over the house attached to bells and buzzers and such. Before bed he'd go around connecting all his traps and trips. She daren't leave the bed during the night for fear of setting off the Royal Symphony percussion section. He had money, you see, and men with money became a little insane with old age. Or perhaps he'd always been a nutcase. She wasn't to know. It was during their second month together that he caught his first intruder. A foolhardy housebreaker had made his way into their home through a conservatory window. He'd taken a false step and, wallop—the bells of St. Mary's. Robert was on him with a truncheon within seconds but the poor chap was too deaf and disoriented to fight him off.

Inspired by his success, Robert had turned to more lethal toys. At the pinnacle of his obsession he'd wired a shotgun to the underside of the living room table attached to a long trip wire. Nobody was surprised when Edna found him the following morning with a big hole in his head. She took sleeping pills and wore ear plugs and had heard nothing. The police assumed he'd been testing his device and failed to get out of the way in time. You could always rely on the English police to come to obvious conclusions. The young constable had put his arms around Edna and consoled her. She seemed to recall the young fellow had a significant erection as he squeezed the sobbing and scantily clad young bride to his chest.

Which brought her succinctly to the other sound. It was a rustle from the twenty-year-old Christmas paper she used to line the bedroom drawers. There was a slight squeak. He'd reached the second drawer from the bottom. All he'd find there were memories. He probably wouldn't linger long enough to appreciate the value and vintage of her undergarments. There was a lot of Marks and Spencer's stuff in there now but in the old days she bought to highlight her curves. She still had it back then. Oh, sir, did she have it and had no problems with flaunting it. Naturally, she didn't have much cause to wear it now. A ninety-year-old in open-crutch panties turned more stomachs than heads but she didn't have the heart to discard her man-hunting underwear.

Her daring attire had put more than a few feathers in her cap. Her fourth husband, George was a perfect example. She'd taken to wearing inappropriate dresses as she walked along the front at Brighton. March was always a good month. The winds off the Channel came in gusts. You could stroll along the promenade and be certain of giving at least a dozen old bench-squatters a quick accidental flash. It wasn't your looks or your walk that won them. It was the racy knickers you wore beneath a simple, seemingly conservative pink dress, every dirty old man's fantasy. Men were so terribly predictable in that respect.

On her return stroll on one particular day, George had hobbled up to her with a walking stick in each hand and introduced himself. He was seventy but still had enough breath to flirt. By June they were wed and by August the poor man had expired of an unexplained respiratory condition.

The cold from the bathroom tiles had already worked its way through her flannelette nightdress and into her bones. She tutted once more at her rash decision not to put on her dressing gown. It was May. Not the absolute coldest month in Melbourne but cool enough. There was even frost on the front lawn. But it was supposed to have been just a brisk scurry down the hallway, up with the nightie, brave the cold seat, a quick wee, and a trot back to bed. She'd even pulled up the quilt to maintain what little heat her seven-stone body had invested there. She laughed silently. It was clearly a plot orchestrated by her body parts. They'd ganged up on her to bring about her downfall. Her bladder was the ringleader. It had lured her into the bathroom, the scene of the crime. She'd fulfilled her obligation to it, washed her hands and switched off the light. That's when she'd heard the cistern. She turned back to do her magic on the handle and there, that simple action had done her in. No more muscle involved than the scratch of a nose but enough to herniate a disk. As all victims will concede, there is no agony-free position into which to contort one's body when one herniates a disk. All she could do was collapse onto the ground like a half-empty sack of hinges. It wasn't the first time her backbone had slipped out of alignment. In her seventies she'd spent most of one year flat on the floor popping muscle relaxants as if they were Jaffas. But here she was without a painkiller in sight. Just brushing the hair back from her eyes sent mule kicks the length of her spine. There was nothing to do but lay and wait, and reminisce. She recalled the first time her spine had rebelled.

Wimbledon had been on the wireless and Angela Mortimer was doing spiffingly well. So all the girls put on their little white skirts and plimsolls and rushed off to the local council courts to emulate their heroine. Edna was no tennis stylist.

She barely left the base line and had no lob shots or spins in her arsenal but little got past her. Rallies ended with ennui rather than winners. Her service was a sight to behold. She tossed the ball so high it often collected moisture from the low-hanging clouds. Not surprisingly it was during a service game that her back first went into spasm. A charming retired doctor two courts down came to her rescue. He manipulated her onto her feet and she manipulated him into her well-trafficked marriage bed. Sadly, two months later, the man was hit by an unidentified automobile and had died on his way to hospital.

Edna was losing the feeling in her fingers and she was certain the chattering of her teeth could be heard in the next room. Dying from the cold wasn't out of the question. It wasn't the way she'd imagined meeting her maker. She'd rather seen herself sliced into segments by a helicopter whilst sky diving or shot in a police pursuit. To keep herself occupied she reached for the small fluffy non-slip mat inside the bathroom door and quietly unpeeled it from the two-sided tape that adhered it to the tiles. The intruder had reached her wardrobe. She heard the empty hangers clang together. She'd only recently sent her annual turf-out to the Opportunity Shop. The crinkle of the plastic-covered cocktail dresses, the clomping of her high-heeled shoes. He was getting closer. Was that a zipper? Was he looking in her boots? Not a bad place to hide money but no prize there today, young man.

She'd been wearing the boots when Geoffrey first came to call. Those were the days before policemen carried name

31

cards. He'd written his name and number on the back of a gas bill. He'd told her he was sorry half a dozen times. He'd heard that three of her husbands had died under mysterious circumstances. He bemoaned her awfully bad luck. But he'd been told by his chief inspector to look into what he called 'statistically unlikely occurrences'. The inefficient system was working in her favour. She'd wondered what the statistical odds would have looked like if they'd discovered the other four deceased husbands. Chiefly to keep Sergeant Geoffrey off her case she'd married and disposed of him too. It was a pity. She'd rather liked him. She'd been very fond of England as well, but to use the appropriate vernacular, the heat was on and she had to flee the scene.

An advertisement in the Observer had pointed to the escape route. "Come to Australia" it had said, "And start your life anew." It was exactly what she needed, a new life and assisted passage to the colonies. Of course she had a sizeable nest egg at that stage and could have traveled on a luxury ocean liner to the other side of the world, but the Aussies were offering to subsidize her trip in order to replenish the big island with suitably pink people. She was certain she'd be lost in the paperwork. She didn't have any skills other than the assassination of men, which she didn't think to mention on the application form but they accepted her anyway.

So began her new life, a house in the most exclusive suburb and a social circle. They treated her like a duchess so she started acting like one. In all her forty-odd years at the earth's extremity she'd only lost four husbands and one of those, Oliver, the ultimate, had succumbed to natural *causes. She'd been tempted to bump him off on a number of occasions but there had been tremendous advances in crime fighting over the years and she doubted she still had the acumen to outsmart the law. Plus, there was the fact that she was no longer the temptress she'd once been. She was afraid she'd terminate one husband too many and be left all alone and desperate in the world . . . just like she was now. She'd arrived at 2008 and was ashamed to admit that it had been twenty-three years since she'd last done anyone in. She missed those good old days. Her life had lost its excitingly destructive edge.*

And here the perfect opportunity to make up for lost time had presented itself. An intruder had broken into her house while she was in the bathroom. She had every right to brain him with a poker or stab him through the heart with a sharpened knitting needle. Nobody would blame her. She might even be lauded in the local press. But what happened? Incapacitated on the bathroom floor without a blunt instrument in sight. With a great deal of effort she might just have been able to reach the loofah, yet no method of turning it into a lethal weapon came to mind. The best a loofah would get you—wielded at ankle height—was very clean shins. Of course he might have died laughing. That was one method she had yet to attempt.

And just as she was planning how she might turn defense into attack the toilet unfurled its final treachery. The cistern gurgled and burped and for reasons only forty-year-old plumbing would be able to disclose, it stopped refilling. The handle clicked loudly and the entire unit sighed. Of all the marvelous timing . . . She was undone.

She hurried to unstick the last corner of the rug from its tile and flipped the shaggy beast over. The sudden movement seemed to drag a length of rusty barbed wire along her backbone and tears filled her eyes. The entire house was holding its breath. She could hear the patterns on the kitchen crockery and the cushions on the sofa but she could not hear the intruder in her bedroom.

One floorboard along the hallway had a mournful groan that she'd never bothered to cure. The sound of that floorboard would signal that the invader had heard the toilet handle and was on his way. Yet she rather savoured the rush of adrenalin. It reminded her of the moments leading up to her putting a hole in Robert's forehead with his own shotgun, the night she'd smothered George with a pillow and that gloriously sunny autumn day she'd driven the Austin over the doctor. Yes, this was what she missed.

The floorboard creaked.

"So, what do you make of it?"

Senior Sergeant Mahon was leaning against the door jamb. Tom Nguyen the medical examiner was hunched over the bodies.

"Buggered if I know, Sarj. You'd need CSI Miami in to work this one out."

"Well, let's assume they're busy and I'm lumbered with you. Give me a guess."

"All right." Nguyen rolled the teenager's head to one side. "This lowlife obviously cracked his head open on the tiles. I'd say he more-than-likely skidded on that thing and sent it flying."

He nodded towards the little white rug now draped over the toilet like a judge's lopsided wig.

"Went arse over apex by the looks of him."

"That's a medical term?"

"It's in the book."

"What about the old girl?"

"Your guess is as good as mine."

"Remind me again why you blokes get paid so much."

"All right, look. It was cold last night. Four degrees and frost. If I'd found her here by herself I'd have assumed she died of exposure. She's hardly dressed for the temperature and she doesn't have a lot of meat on her. But it doesn't explain why she's cuddled up to the boy."

"Body heat?"

"Could be, but I'd warrant he wasn't alive for long once he cracked his head open."

The Senior Sergeant was distracted by a movement behind him. He turned to see his constable standing in the hall.

"Sarj," she said. "Gotta minute?"

He followed her to the back bedroom where cabinet drawers hung open and dresses had been pulled from a wardrobe and left in a heap. The constable directed his attention to the bed where the top mattress had been slid half-off to reveal a base that probably didn't do anything for the old lady's posture. Inside the box-frame was a neat brickwork of leaf-green hundred-dollar notes all tied in bundles.

"Holy baloney!" said the sergeant. "Was this the way you found it?"

"Haven't touched a thing."

The senior sergeant prized out one of the wads. It was at least two hundred bills thick.

"Jesus," he said. "How's your maths?"

"Shithouse, but I know there has to be a couple of million here."

"Then I guess we know what the young thug in the bathroom was looking for."

"You think he killed her, Sarj?"

"That's for Tom to say. All I know is that sad old girls like that are always going to be the victim in this world."

"No argument there, Sarj."

A Night on the Tiles

Like Edna in this story, I fled England for the imagined sun/beach/surf lifestyle in Australia. I'd trained as a physical education teacher in Berkshire where the three seasons were; cold, wet, and depressing. I couldn't imagine a life of standing out in the drizzle, my tracksuit sodden and clingy, watching little boys run around in their damp shorts (although I subsequently met men who fantasized about that very thing). So I made passage to Sydney. It rained for the entire first month I was there.

I did one or two peculiar jobs before working with refugees which led me to Asia (A very long story told in sixteen words). I met people from all around the world, most of whom had their own reasons for being in Australia; escaping war, poverty or persecution. Others were there escaping bad weather and boredom. Everywhere I went, I met English people who thought it was their country and the Aussies were blooming lucky to be allowed to stay there. And I met rich English widows who took tea at The Opera House and kept their pasts to themselves. But there was an unmistakable glint in their eyes.

This is one of my favourites in the collection and I think it would make a nice little Independent film. So, if you're reading this, Mr. Eastwood ....

JACK WONG HAS A RARE MOMENT OF LUCIDITY

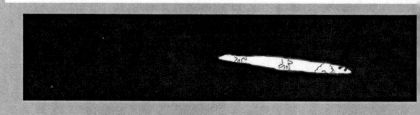

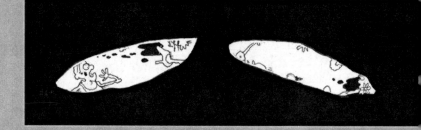

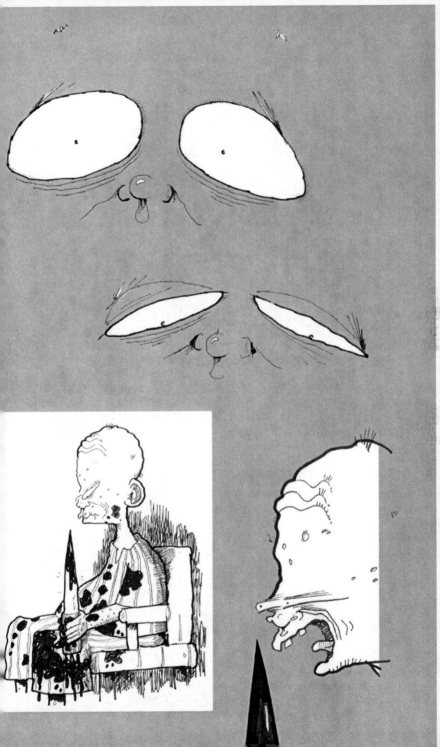

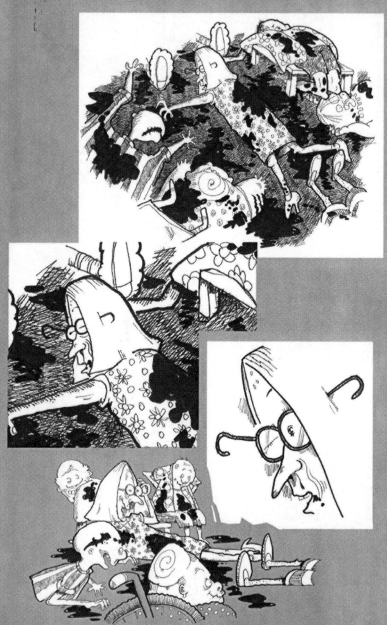

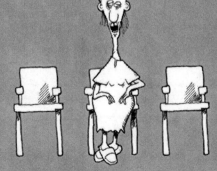

ETHEL
APPLEYARD
ENJOYS A
RARE MOMENT
OF LUCIDITY

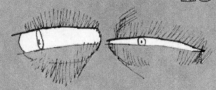

Jack Wong Has a Rare Moment of Lucidity.

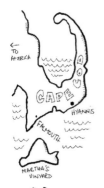

In 1975 I worked on a summer programme for intellectually handicapped adults in Cape Cod, Massachusetts. People who had been institutionalized all their lives, more for the way they looked than for the threat they posed to society, were selected from their respective cuckoo's nests and given a week's holiday on the coast.

For many, it was their first vacation. I was one of four counselors whose mission was to "show them a good time." I was their McMurphy. We bowled, fished, disco'd, played ball, hiked, swam and ate out. It was the best summer of my life and I was paid for it.

Everywhere we went, people would come up to us and ask where we were from. I was never the person they asked. I suppose I looked like one of the loonier members of the group.

I recall one young lady called Alice who used to slide in and out of consciousness from time to time. She'd be perfectly normal one minute—comatose the next. Most of our holiday groups enjoyed a good joke and one of the lads, knowing Alice would soon be rejoining us, suggested we should all play dead. So we did. Well, why not? There were too many gigglers in the group to give Alice a real fright, but she had a good chuckle. I just took it up another peg in this story. Bad taste? Why not?

COUNSELOR

Tart

"YOU THINK SHE'S there now?"

"As far as I know, dad."

"Well, I'm not having it. I'm not."

My father had put on and taken off his Maroubra Seals waterproof jacket six times since I'd arrived. It was currently hanging off one shoulder like a shedding skin.

"Bert wasn't that pleased about it himself," I told him.

"I don't give a fat flying fart what Bert's pleased or not pleased about. He gets pleasure watching info-bloody-mercials, that man. What would he know about anything important? It's her I'm worried about. I mean, bugger it, there's danger involved. I'm going over there."

He didn't make any effort to right his jacket or head for the door. He perched his rear end against the kitchen table and adopted his, 'Look out. I'm really angry' face. It used to scare the shit out of me when I was three but I'm fifty now and it looks more like he's suffering from angina. He probably is.

"I don't think it'll do you any good," I told him. "Looks like she's made up her mind."

"It's immoral."

My dad was hardly the one to talk about morals. He'd left his morals rolled up on the floor beside the bed of half the married women on our street when he was in his prime. He did so many home visits someone once asked mum if he was a meter reader for New South Wales Electric. But he wasn't in the market for a lecture, not now. And I wasn't in a position to give him one.

"No, I mean (he was still working on his phrasing) disgusting. That's what it is. Disgusting. Worse than immoral. Perverted and sick."

I was starting to wonder what sort of vocabulary he'd need to amass before he'd actually go off and do something about it.

"It was her choice," I reminded him.

"Yeah, and we all know how good your mother is at making choices."

I resisted the obvious rejoinder. Instead of baiting him I looked around at the kitchen I'd eaten in for the first seventeen years of my life. Nothing had really changed. He was still making the effort. The Victoria Bitter crate by the back door was covered with a flowery tea towel. The windows had been wiped over from the inside. There were dishes pretending to be drying on the draining board, two of his best plates. He did all his eating at the Seals and he couldn't make toast without a recipe book open so I couldn't imagine why he'd need an eighteen inch dinner set, two dessert bowls, two sets of cutlery and a pair of wine glasses, unless he was setting me up, wanting me to think he wasn't a lonely old bastard. I knew otherwise.

"And just what type of men . . . you know?"

I could tell he was distressed. He kept reaching to his back pocket where the coffin nails had lived for all those years, till he got the ultimatum. 'Quit or cough up dry blood for a month then die a horrid slow death.' He'd had to think about that one. He'd anguished over the choice for almost a week. It could have gone either way. He settled in the end for life with an increased quota of beer to make up for the inconvenience. He still looked like something out of a Tim Burton movie but he wasn't wheezing any more. He could make it down to the car without sitting on the steps half way. There were times I wanted to kiss him for showing me what I'd turn out like if I'd lived his life.

"Young, she said," I told him.

"Young? Young?"

"That's what she said. Young and good looking most of 'em."

If his arteries had still been clogged I imagined that might have been the moment he'd keel over and carry his ethereal bedpan to the big dunny just outside heaven. Even in his improved state of health the grey still drained from his face and left him looking like a carved clay pipe.

"Am I missing something here?" he asked. I'd never heard him do soprano before. "Am I? I ask in all seriousness. Your mother is—and, no disrespect intended here. She's still a fine looking girl . . ." He stood, took of his jacket and threw it across the table. It knocked over the little basket of plastic flowers that had graced the kitchen since the first world war. ". . . but she is a considerable way down the hill, boy."

He called me boy when he was feeling inferior.

"In my day," he continued, "a chook over fifty could barely hope to get a smile out of her husband. As they say in the cruder parts of town, she couldn't even give it away."

"Let alone sell it," I helped.

"I don't see a need for crudity."

"Sorry."

"So, as I've obviously been in hibernation since the world changed, pray tell me what happened to alter that state of affairs."

"The internet," I told him.

Usually you could drop the words 'the internet' into a conversation and it would explain everything. But dad was one of those cavemen who thought WWW was a cable wrestling channel. He didn't know computer from calamari. Naturally, he'd never admit that.

"Oh yes?" he said. "And what particular department of the internet are we referring to here?

"The porn sites, dad."

He liked to turn on indignation when I mentioned pornography despite the fact that I'd known since the age of eleven where he kept his stash of Sexpapers. He subscribed and had them delivered once a week in a brown wrapper.

"And what does filthy porn have to do with your mother?"

"Here we go then," I thought. To delay the moment I sat on the stool and prized the lid off the biscuit tin. I was hoping for Tim Tams. All he had were Gingernuts. I hated Gingernuts.

"I'm waiting," he said.

"You aren't going to like it."

"I already don't like it. It couldn't get much worse."

"All right. The internet has had the effect of bringing like-minded souls together. In many cases this is a good thing. A fossilized turd collector in Latvia can chat with turd fossil fanciers all around the world at the click of a mouse. Good for him. Good for the world. No harm done. But then there's the dark side. Let's say old Kye Kinkersen in outer Denmark reaches the age of forty deeply ashamed that he has sexual feelings for seven-year-old boys. Quite rightly, he suppresses these urges and remains independently depressed, destined to jump under a train before he's sixty. Good for us. Good for the world.

"But then he's on the web and he stumbles across a site where a whole community of middle-aged cretins with sexual feelings for seven-year-old boys hangs out. They have a club and a logo. T-shirts. They exchange pictures and experiences and contacts. Kye suddenly isn't ashamed any more. He's got pals. He thinks he's normal. If it's on the internet it must be a legitimate hobby. He gets his club key chain and he moves up to Level Two. He's back in the game. Kye's exonerated."

"Bastards."

"Which brings us to mum," I continued. "On the web you'll find sites that classify themselves as MILF. It stands for, 'Mothers I'd like to . . .' and I'll let you fill in the last blank for yourself. And those sites attract all the blokes with mother fetishes. They have a thing for the more mature lady. Perhaps they had fantasies about their own mothers when they were growing up."

"Perverts."

"Quite so. But it was only a matter of time—seconds if you consider the pace of developments on the net—before MILF branched off into GILF. And all the men out there with elderly lady fetishes came out of the World Wide Woodwork."

"Wait! Are you saying your mother was involved in one of these web things?" Dad's fists were clenched.

"She didn't need to be. Following the new trends in perversion, the local brothels expanded in weird directions. They started to get requests for more mature ladies and the madams came out of retirement. It was a granny renaissance. They found themselves with more work than they could handle. So they advertised."

"And Nora . . . ?"

I hadn't heard dad use mum's name since they were still together.

"She answered the ad from a place called, Tenderly Massage. They're in the union. It appears they have excellent remuneration, health benefits, dental discounts. They've got . . ."

"It's prostitution."

"It's legal."

"Legal doesn't necessarily mean right. She was a dispatcher for General Motors for thirty years. What does she know about whoring?"

"From what they told her at the orientation it appears there's not much to know. Most of the customers just want a little bit of old-fashioned discipline from granny and a . . ."

My dad put his hands over his ears and started to hum something that sounded like "Help is on its Way" by the Little River Band, but it was hard to tell. Dad never could carry a tune. I assumed he didn't want to hear the details. His eyes reflected the light from the backyard. That wouldn't have happened if they'd been dry. He frowned and his unkempt eyebrow hair fanned out like the tails of albino peacocks.

"Son, I don't get it," he said. "What's happened to her? Why's she doing this?"

"I guess it's the freedom," I told him. "You make odd decisions when you find yourself out of your chains. I remember doing a lot of odd shit when I left home and went off to Uni. For mum, I don't know. This is the first time she's been independent since she met you. You and her were married for . . ."

"Thirty-six years."

I looked at him and smiled. He blushed. I got the feeling he could have tallied the remaining months, days, and—with a brief glance at the Rugby League commemorative clock—the seconds they'd been together . . . and apart.

"And on the very day she walked out on you . . ."

"We separated."

"Right. but on that self-same day, she moved in with Bert."

"Talk about bad decisions."

"Barely an hour of freedom between the two regimes. Then, after I don't know how many years of excruciating boredom with Bert, *Home and Away* and *Neighbours* on prime time, crossword puzzles and *Trivial Pursuit*, and holdy-hand walks round the shops at Maroubra Junction, something finally happens to make her up and leave that lump of wood and move out by herself."

"Yeah, courage by the semi-trailer-load all of a sudden," dad spat out. "Where did that come from I'd like to know? And when did all this sexual electricity suddenly start coursing through her veins? She didn't even use to . . ."

He censored himself there. Remembered who he was talking to, I bet. Mother-father confidentiality. I went in for the kill.

"I heard you were responsible."

"Me?"

"That's what I heard."

"Rack off. I've barely said a word to her for years."

"The Seals calendar?"

A strange quiet filled the kitchen like a car airbag inflating. Dad slowly retrieved his jacket, pulled it on and tried to match the zipper with its track.

"What about it?"

"The word on the street is that you put mum's name forward for it."

"You've been walking down some funny streets, boy."

"Gary Thackray told me."

"He's eighty. He can't remember what hole to spoon his lunch into."

"You're on the club committee together."

"I . . . I can't recall whose names I put in."

"He says you only submitted one . . . mum's."

"Well, if I did it would have been for a lark."

"But she did it, didn't she."

Dad sighed.

"I would never have thought it," he said to the zip.

"You put mum's name forward as one of twelve senior lady club members who'd be bold enough to appear on a nude calendar. Nude, Dad! At her age?"

"Helen Mirren did it."

"Helen Mirren's an actress."

"It was a fundraiser. A bit of fun. Other clubs were doing it. And like I say, I didn't think she'd go for it."

"But she did. October. Nothing but a cricket bat between her and the full Monty. Your ex-wife. My mother. Exposed in public."

"It ended up embarrassing me more than her by the looks of it."

"She says it was liberating. Made her rethink."

"Rethink what?"

"Her sexuality."

"Wait! Are you trying to tell me her appearing on a soft nude calendar turned her into a hooker?"

"She got a lot of compliments. More than a few offers, if you know what I mean."

"No!"

"Bloody oath. It gave her a new self-image. By putting mum's name down for the calendar, you were indirectly responsible for freeing her from her inhibitions."

Dad took off his jacket and laid it over the back of the chair. It slid off like a silk nightie and dropped to the floor. He didn't seem to notice. He walked to the sink and turned on a tap presumably just to see whether water came out of it. It did. He turned it off and stared out at the Russian elm in the middle of the yard surrounded by all the ghosts of the flowers that once played there.

"So, you're telling me . . ." he said, his face was taut and angular like plastic surgery performed by a carpenter. "You're telling me I'm responsible for all this?"

"I wouldn't go that far," I told him.

"Just how far *would* you go?"

"I'd say, ooh, I don't know. I'd say the desire was probably there. The passion was inside her. She'd always wondered what it would be like, you know? But it took a big spoon to crack open that shell of hers. You just handed her the spoon."

Dad turned back to the sink and reached for the tap again, but before he had a chance to splash water onto his face I caught the tears. Those damp eyes were leaking without a doubt. Wonders would never cease. They'd be declaring Melbourne a no-beer zone next.

"You think she's there now?" he asked again, wiping his face with the dishcloth.

"As far as I know, dad."

"She hasn't started . . . ?"

"They said the mornings are slack."

"Right. I suppose they would be."

It suddenly seemed really urgent for him to be out of the unit. He told me to be sure to flick the catch on the lock before I left but I could stay as long as I liked. Watch some TV. Beer in the esky. Have a lay-down if I wanted. My dad and I weren't the touchy feely type but before he left he put a hand on my shoulder. It was tentative like a teenager's first grope of his girlfriend's knee. It probably meant something but, for the life of me, I couldn't work out what. He smiled, and left me in the kitchen with my uneaten Gingernut in my hand. When I heard the front door shut, I got up from the stool and picked up my old man's jacket from the floor.

I have no idea why my mum stayed in love with my dad for all those years. He was a shit. I have to assume it's got something to do with smell. Penguins travel for months and choose a mate from the scent. Then they stay mates for life. It has nothing to do with whether the male looks good with his shirt off or does Elvis impersonations. It's all preprogrammed in their beaks. I guess Mum had no choice. Dad was up her nose. I sometimes wonder whether she chose brain-dead Bert as her retreat because he was one of the few men who wouldn't have put up a fight to keep her. Dad just had to say the word and Bert would have let her go, driven her to our place in his Morris Traveler, sat and had a beer with dad while she unpacked. But dad never said the word. Probably didn't know what it was.

And mum waited. She knew dad was deficient in matters of the heart. She wasn't expecting Hallmark, just a sniff. They bumped into each other at the club every week but Sydney Seals was a sprawling party of a place. Two people could remain distant there for twenty years. And that's what had happened with mum and dad. Who could know whether the old fellow put mum's name down for the calendar out of spite or jealousy or desperation at his inability to force kind words out of himself, or whether it really was just a lark? But mum recognized it as his submission. It was the invitation she'd been waiting for. She threw off her prim and her proper and her Marks and Spencer's undies and bore all for the camera. And it really did change her. I saw the difference.

I'd given her my blessing for the nude project. I'm not sure why. Perhaps I'd felt the glow in her heart when she came to ask me. I hadn't seen that spirit in her since I was little. She got a lot of social mileage out of the calendar and it was inevitable that Bert wouldn't be able to keep up with her new self. I hadn't been surprised in the least when she told me about her bachelor pad or that she'd thrown out all her old clothes.

She started dressing like the wife of a professional foot-baller. But the news of her new career move caught me with my pants down.

I remember I was having lunch with her at Wolfie's Grill at the Rocks. I had a vague feeling my mouth was hanging open. I recall wondering who this elegant old lady was and why she was talking porn between dainty mouthfuls of prawn cocktail. She'd told it pretty much the way I'd passed it on to dad but her version was a lot saucier. I'd left out a lot of the juice for obvious reasons. She went through it in detail from the spread of internet perversion through the offer from Tenderly Massage and details of what she was supposed to do for the clients. Only the ending was different.

She'd smiled and asked, "What do you think?"

What did I think? I'd stopped thinking somewhere around 'seven-year-old boys' and started to hyper-ventilate. My seventy-year-old mother had spent fifteen minutes calmly explaining why she was about to take a job at a high-class brothel in a suburb that made muggers so nervous they walked around in pairs. The lady who'd held my clammy little hand and walked me to primary school explaining the psychology of bullies and how it was alright to hit them back, wanted to know what I thought about her rolling around on greasy sheets with perverts? I smiled and looked over her shoulder.

"All right, I get it. Where is it?"

"What, love?"

"The camera."

She seemed truly bemused and I knew instantly we weren't on a TV reality set up. This was spontaneous reality. The real type. The worst kind.

"Mum," I said. "I think all those gin and tonics at the club have finally eaten a hole right through your brain."

She'd giggled and a sparkle filled her eyes like champagne bubbles.

"Oh, I am pleased," she'd said.

"Pleased?"

A prawn was skewered at the end of my fork and was enjoying his last amusement park ride. I was waving him this way and that as I listed all the reasons why mum's decision was the silliest bloody thing I'd heard in my life. "What," I asked, in conclusion, "could you possibly be pleased about?"

That's when I got the different ending.

You see? Mum was pleased because I'd believed every word of the cock-and-bull story she'd spun me. It was a corker. It was a presentation worthy of an Oscar. A Golden Gullible. The Nobel Prize for prefabrication. I was astounded and immensely proud that my mother had invested so much time and effort into researching such an elaborate porky. She had no intention of selling her lollies to unwashed perverts with dole money in their pockets. She merely wanted the concept to sound viable. She was pleased because if she could suck me in there was a very good chance my dad would fall for it too.

I don't know what'll come of this. I've been known to tell a few tales myself. I think dad believed me. Mum's spending the day parked out front of Tenderly Massage in her old rust gold Holden. She has that worked out too. As soon as she sees my dad's cream Corolla approach she'll get out of her car, grab her dry-cleaned micro-dress in its sheer plastic protection from the back seat, and walk towards the entrance of the parlour in her new stilettos. She has a lot of faith in this plan. In her dream Dad stops his car in the middle of the road, throws open the door and grabs her. He tells her he's never stopped loving her, that he wants her to end all this foolishness, and throws her into the back seat, the dry-cleaning crushed under his rear tyres.

She conceded that the scenario might be more like, he drives past, almost runs her over. He brakes, reverses, and asks her whether she's broken down. She tells him, no, she's going to work. He tells her he's on his way to have a coffee . . . and goes quiet. She says she's got a few minutes free and she was planning on having a coffee, too . . . perhaps . . . ? He looks at her like it hadn't occurred to him but he says, okay. They drive to Toto's Café. They talk.

I had my own scenario in mind. By the time dad gets the car out of the carport his indignation has all but slipped from his shoulders like that nylon jacket. He gets as far as the corner shop and it occurs to him a trip into town uses up an awful lot of petrol. He abandons his plan and goes down the club for a beer instead. That sounds more like dad to me. Deep down, I hope that's the way it turns out.

Tart.

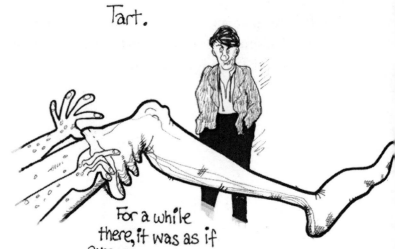

For a while there, it was as if every woman over 50 was whipping off her clothes for this or that charity nude calendar.

There was even a movie about it with Helen Mirren flashing her botty around. And I got to wondering about it. Did 'doing it' change the women? Did the reactions they received have a positive or negative effect on their self esteem. Could it have led to nude modelling? The internet? Sex?

A friend of mine, whom we shall call Rolin, was doing W.W.W. research for this story ("Honestly, Jess. I'm doing research") and came across the MILF phenomenon. Since my work in child protection, I've been very nervous about the internet and the fact that it can make perverts feel good about themselves. But there are some fetishes, although moderately scary (dressing up in gerbil suits??) that don't appear to have victims. A physical attraction to older women seems to have united a whole army of men under one banner. It has to make a woman feel good about herself to be courted doesn't it? I know my mum gets a thrill out of admiring glances she elicits at car boot sales and whistles at buildin sites. But she predates P.C.

The One-Legged Marathon Runner of 12B Wildebeest Crescent

"SIR, WE'D RATHER you didn't do that."

"What? What are you talking about, girl?"

"You were rearranging the books."

"I most certainly was not."

"Sir, we have a CCTV camera up there in the corner."

"Oh, you do, do you? Well regardless of the fact that I don't recall giving you my permission to film me shopping . . ."

"We don't have to . . ."

"Regardless of that fact, I strongly suggest you get your spy cam adjusted so that it's able to discern between a gentleman contemplating a purchase and a common vandal."

The morbidly gothic sales clerk clawed forward two paperbacks with her long black fingernails. Revealed, was the latest in the Cakes Copeland series, *The Ice-cream Lady of Angkor Wat.*

"You put these paperbacks here," she said.

"I did not."

"I was watching you. You carried a dozen books over from the two-for-one stack and lined them up to hide the Copelands."

"To hide the . . . ? Don't be ridiculous. I . . . I merely forgot where I'd picked them up from. I'm a senior citizen. We elderly people have poor memories. It's an affliction you'll no doubt incur when all that leaden eye-gunk starts to soak though to your brain in a year or two."

"No need to get personal."

"You're accusing me of reckless rearrangement. That isn't personal?"

"It's not an accusation. It's recorded. You want to see the tape?"

"Oho, summon the police, Vampira. I think you'll discover that librarianship isn't yet a criminal offence in Scotland. Go ahead, call them."

"I don't need to. All I have to do is tell you to leave."

"Really? And do you honestly suppose your manager will allow you to eject me from a store I have been frequenting for half a century?"

"For your information, I'm the manager and I've never seen you here before in my life."

"You're the what? How old are you? Twelve?"

"Look . . . sir. Are you planning to buy any of these? If not . . ."

She began to gather the copies of Andrew Mc-Creadie Jones' *The One-legged Marathon Runner of 12B*

Wildebeest Crescent that the old fellow had lined up in pairs along the eye-level shelf.

"Well I tell you, lassie, if I were going to buy a crime novel it would certainly be one of these McCreadie Jones rather than the Copeland rubbish. What on earth are his books doing up there on such prime browsing real estate?"

She ignored him and carried the Joneses back to the fifty-percent table. He shuffled after her, his plastic raincoat swishing like a kung fu sound effect on a cheap video.

"Look, you're starting to give me the willies," she said.

"Is that so? Well, we certainly wouldn't want you having any willies, would we now? I tell you what. You answer my question and I'll cease to haunt your day. I'll crawl back to the street with all the other vermin."

She turned to him and pursed her seemingly bruised lips. "Really? All right. What was the question?"

"It would appear all that coffin time has bunged up your ears with damp earth. Very well, I'll speak slowly." He picked up one of the McCreadie Jones she'd just restacked. "Explain to me why literature such as this is condemned to the bottom of the bargain basement barrel when tacky dross like Copeland's is allowed a place of honour?"

"I answer that and you'll go?"

"I swear on your grave."

"Okay. Copeland is shit hot right now. I can't keep the books on the shelves. I can't keep up with the orders. This lot will be gone by the weekend."

"But why? They're set in . . . in a place nobody could hope to locate on a map."

"Cambodia."

"Oh. You know that, do you? They hardly seem your style. Don't tell me you've read them?"

"And I'm very fond of them. They're exotic and dynamic. He makes me want to go there. His characterizations are rich and credible."

The old man laughed rudely.

"You're just reciting the publisher's press notice," he sneered.

"I am not."

"Well, they say exactly the same thing about the McCreadie Jones.' "

"Who does? They're ancient. I've read a couple of them. Nothing ever happens. They're books for people who don't need a life. Burundi? I mean, honestly, who gives a toss about Burundi?"

"Who gives a . . . ? Well, I tell you, panda eyes, I give a toss. In fact I give a momentous toss. My toss is barely containable. He's an exceptional writer. To tell the truth, it was my intention to buy several copies of his books as gifts. What do you say about that?"

"I say, show me the money."

Andrew McCreadie Jones wiped his feet on the thick bristle door mat and slammed the front door shut behind him.

"Are you not even going to honour me with a greeting?" he called out.

He stood there in the gloomy hallway and listened for a response. The wallpaper looked particularly grey. He recalled a time when the brilliant red tulips positively leaped from their lilac vases. When it was younger, the grandfather clock by the hat stand had emitted a vital tick and a positively grand tock. Now that it was dusty and bronchial it could say only 'thick . . . thock . . . thick', etcetera ad infinitum. The whole house had that same muffled air about it. He hung up his plastic raincoat and walked through to the dark kitchen, a room deprived of daylight by the leafy horse chestnut tree in the back garden. Mama lay as if in a stupor on her blanket and barely raised her head in greeting. Had it really been so many years ago that the old Labrador was as frisky as Jones' public; drooling at his feet, sniffing around his ankles, fascinated by his every action? Could enthusiasm really drain away like adrenal fluid from a leaky gland?

So few letters dropped onto the mat these days. It was all e-mail and blagging and that web nonsense. Nobody took the trouble to write on paper anymore. Nobody appreciated his handwritten responses. It was all instant and unfeeling gratification.

"You're certainly never going to find a computer in my house," he'd told his agent. The look of disappointment rolled over the woman's craggy face like a rain cloud at a picnic.

"But Andy, it's the future," she'd bemoaned. "In fact, it's the present. You're already a decade behind the herd."

He didn't care. He enjoyed grazing alone on the empty plain of the past. He'd performed his book tours diligently and continued to pull in the crowds. He liked the way they aged with him like hand-knitted mufflers. In the early nineties he had still been the undisputed heavyweight champion of the exotic crime cozy. There had been a belief in those days that nobody would ever dethrone him. And then *he* came along: Cakes Copeland. What type of mother would name their child after confectionary? It was a gimmick, of course, just as all the quirky, spirit-worshipping, landmine maimed, uneducated, big hearted, English-speaking characters were gimmicks. Just as the setting was an obvious contrivance. Find a country nobody's been to and make up facts about it. Turn a dull place into a James Joycian Milkwood through the magic of ignorance-exploitation.

Jones was not shy to admit that he knew Burundi. That he was Burundi. He was at one with the people and the culture. He'd lived there in the sixties in the capital, Bujumbura, for two sometimes arduous years as a British volunteer. Those were the early days of Her Majesty's Voluntary Services Overseas. They'd dispatched him to teach geography and calculus at a government high school via his sometimes baffling version of French. Few of the natives had been bold enough to suggest the Scot's accent was less than comprehendible. They all saw it as a failing of their own. After all, the British professor was there under a special agreement with the newly reinstated royal family. King Mwami Mwambutsa the Fourth himself had shaken his hand and thanked him for joining their struggle to unite and educate the Burundian people.

Two years later the royal family was deposed in a violent coup and several decades of tribal massacres began. But that had been neither here nor there to McCreadie Jones. He had his life experience in the bank and returned to teach French at the Gordons in Huntly. He had returned with a compendium of diaries in which, amongst other things, he'd fantasized the thoughts of people around him in Africa. The woman selling yams at the market. The old man who came to repair his overhead fan at a fee equivalent to four pennies in the old currency.

The teacher rewrote his notes as fictional conversations and soon had a premise for a novel. It was what later became known as a 'feel good' story called *The Deputy Food Taster of Burundi*, set amid the relative peace between Belgian occupation and bloodthirsty chaos. It was a feast of a book liberally spiced with humour and emotion and culture and to his great pleasure it was accepted by a medium-sized publishing house in Glasgow.

The book inspired neither love nor hatred from the reviewing community. There were those who wondered how anyone could set a novel in Burundi without even mentioning genocide. But, as Andrew McCreadie Jones pointed out in an early interview, the actual world was already a terribly dour place without reading of natives cutting off each other's heads with machetes. The staff and pupils at Gordons were astounded that such a grim man could produce such a warm and funny novel.

To the publisher's surprise, the reading public took to the book and, over the course of a year, the author became a celebrity. His next three books were devoured. He quit his teaching job and became a full-time writer. He was, they all agreed, the Mwami Mwambutsa the Fourth of his genre—the king alone on the parapet walls of cozy-fiction castle—until *he* came on the scene.

McCreadie Jones poured hot water into his teapot and carried the Derbyshire antique to the table. He let the Earl Grey stew as his mother had taught him and opened the unnecessarily trendy black and white carrier bag. He took out the three bargain copies of his own book and then slowly removed the Copeland. She'd bullied him into it, of course, the ebony-embossed twelve-year-old manager person, black-lipped from the crypt. She'd goaded him.

"You've read him, I assume," she'd said, running her laser stun ray over the books' little rectangular zebra crossings.

"Certainly not," he'd replied.

"How do you know he's crap, then?" She laughed annoyingly. "You're just like my gran, you are."

"I am nothing like your gran."

"Y'are. She gets it into her head she doesn't like a thing and you couldn't drag her to try it with chains and a front-end loader."

So, largely to show her he wasn't at all like her gran, he'd bought a copy of the awful Angkor Wat book. Paid good money for it. He'd contemplated dropping it into the litter bin at the station but the Home Security people would probably arrest him for terrorism. Leaving a boring but ignitable object in a public place. But he knew it was cheap pulp and he'd get a good flame out of it in his hearth. He poured his tea and carried the rattly cup and unwanted book to his dusty armchair. The newspaper was already balled-up on the grate, the sticks rafted out on top of it, and the coal resplendent at the summit. One match, as ever, was all that would be needed to start a blue-ribbon, McCreadie Jones fire.

But first he sat and sipped his tea and his gaze fell upon the blurb on the back cover of the book. His lips lost contact with the china and a little dribble of Earl Grey worked its way down his chin. It was a quotation from the *New York Times*. Not a person. Just the *New York Times*, as if the entire bloody newspaper; the owner, the editors, the sports department and the lady who wheeled around the donut trolley, all emphatically agreed with its sentiment. They'd all sat down at a huge meeting and fine-tuned the wording,

"CAKES COPELAND IS THE UNDISPUTED KING OF THE EXOTIC CRIME COZY."

Despite the thickness of the walls, Mrs. Giles next door heard the cup and saucer shatter against the fireplace. She assumed the old fool was drunk again. It wouldn't be the first time he'd started his one-man wakes before the sun went down. She wouldn't

71

be stopping by to see if he was all right. She hadn't spoken to the grumpy bastard for twenty years.

The turnout at the Aberdeen Town Hall was spectacular. The literary festival had been running for three days and the organizers were delighted to see how the citizens had taken it to their hearts. It was a Wednesday and the balmy July evening had brought out a lively flock of smiling Aberdonians in their short-sleeves and festival T-shirts and little summer dresses. It seemed hardly possible that such gay people might find the time to sit and read a book. But they were a knowledgeable crowd who, when confronted with an esteemed author, avoided such questions as, "Where do you get your ideas from?" and "How much did ye make on your last book, darling?"

Admission to this once-only evening with international best selling author, Cakes Copeland, was by advance booking only. Those who foolishly thought they might sneak in anyway were turned away at the door by a chunky girl with a George Orwell tattoo and the picture of a pig on her bicep. She now stood at the back of the room counting empty seats. The large gentleman in the second row had booked four months earlier on the day it was first announced that Copeland would be attending the festival. He'd phoned once a week since to confirm that his name was still on the list.

"But, sir, I've already told you it . . ."

"Don't give me a hard time. Just check it."

He'd arrived at the town hall two hours earlier

and sat patiently on his seat clutching a trendy black-and-white carrier bag. Andrew McCreadie Jones was bearded now and unkempt. He'd taken to eating rubbish from the fast food joints, the instant rubbish you pay for as opposed to the rubbish you help yourself to from the skip out the back. That isn't to say the skip selection is any less nutritious. He'd started to drink again and his clothes had that brawny rye-tweed smell you associate with homeless men who live on park benches. The people seated on either side of him were leaning rather obviously into their partners. The George Orwell girl had considered not letting him in but—although his personal hygiene was in doubt—he seemed to be sober and well behaved. He sat on his allotted seat wearing dark glasses, clutching his carrier bag, a cheeky secretive smile on his lips. An eccentric artist-type. Festivals like this had to expect the odd weirdo.

The audience rhubarb subsided like a noisy wave snuffed out on the sand when the interviewer, a well-known Scottish television news presenter, walked casually up to the platform. He was followed by an elegant, middle-aged gentleman with a controlled five o'clock shadow. The onlookers knew from his book jacket photos that this was Cakes Copeland and when he flashed his well-practiced smile at them they let him see their own dentistry in return. All but McCreadie Jones who kept his tobacco-stained teeth to himself. The two men sat in large, over-stuffed armchairs. Festivals liked to do that, set up the stage as if these were two fellows having a little powwow in the privacy of their own living room. They called it, "In Conversation" and forced you to loosen your tie and carry a coffee mug. It might have worked except there were seven hundred people there gawking at you and there could never be anything relaxed or natural about your chat.

Copeland was an American, so there was something tense about his casual look. A Scot would have sat there in his brown cardigan and his black-rimmed glasses with a pink plaster on the hinge. He'd probably have a bit of dog shit on the soul of his shoe held up for all to see. But there was nothing accidental about the author from around the world. McCreadie Jones had assumed the jacket pictures had been airbrushed but it was clear it was the man himself who'd been touched up; designer smile wrinkles, a loose strand of hair, not quite over the eye, shirt-sleeves rolled up to exactly the same point on each arm, socks without holes. He seemed to be doing everything he possibly could to make the old man hate him.

Since that rainy day back in February when his mother's last bone china teacup and saucer hit the wall, McCreadie Jones had known what needed to be done. It was as clear as Glenfiddich, as obvious as the red bulb at the end of his nose. There could no sooner be two kings of the genre than there could be two lions leading a pride. This was a matter of honour. Something had shorted in the complicated circuit board of his mind that day. The *New York Times* had rained on his exposed elements and left him smoking.

In the sixties, British airports hadn't expected passengers to be arriving with weapons in their suitcases. Apart from the fact that it just wasn't polite to import firepower, they tended to assume that there had already been some cursory inspection of baggage at the point of departure. The security detail at the Bujumbura airport in 1965 was a young lady who'd recently graduated from McCreadie Jones' calculus class at the government high school. She didn't care at all that he might have had a Mac-50 and forty rounds of ammunition in his bag. She was just glad to see the back of him.

Everyone with money had a gun in Burundi. There was always that tingly feeling that somebody might climb in through the window and slice off your arm. The head of the school had presented it to his new teacher with the same nonchalance with which he'd handed over the keys to the washroom. McCreadie Jones had never shot anyone. He'd waved the gun around threateningly on a number of occasions and once made a hole in his own ceiling, but the old French pistol had no kills to its name. Mrs. Giles next door had come very close to being his first victim on one occasion when she refused to cut back her ugly sycamore which was dropping its seed pods on McCreadie Jones' turnip patch and denying them what little sun the country could muster. At that time he'd been too drunk to recall where he'd stashed his bullets. Drink makes a poor assassin. But he was in control of himself now. The jungle would soon be his once more to prowl alone.

He reached into the carrier bag and was surprised at how warm the metal felt. Something dispensing death so instantaneously should surely have been cold–old-blooded, shudderingly, icily sinister. Instead it was room temperature like an unplugged curling tong. He slid his hand from the bag and waited. Q and A. His turn: "Would you agree that Andrew McCreadie Jones is still the undisputed king of the exotic crime cozy?"

The disquieting American would answer in a snide, roundabout way. He'd be falsely modest, say, "Jones was pretty good but times have changed. People's reading tastes have become influenced by television and the internet." Hand in bag. Flash of room-temperature metal. BANG! Wrong answer. "Who was that bearded avenger? Was it Zorro? The Lone Ranger? No," they'll all say, "it was McCreadie Jones, the king of the jungle." Up on the litter, borne to the front of the gathering of medicine men, the buffalo-horn crown placed on his head, all drop to their knees. All hail McCreadie Jones.

But he waited for his time and suffered the show, dross, cheap wit, smartarse responses, flirtation with the lass in barely a margin of a skirt off to the left, name dropping, pseudo-intelligent references to US foreign policy and history that he'd probably looked up on his precious internet just before he left his hotel suite this evening. Then, like the slow train from Huntly to Aberdeen, it arrived, twenty minutes of question time. McCreadie Jones threw up his hand.

Even though his own arm had been much slower into the air the mayor was allowed the privilege of asking the initial question. He was a big man with the voice of a sparrow.

"One thing that's always astounded me," he said, his pitch somewhere between speaker static and a fork sliding off a tin roof, "is how you were able to create a genre all by yourself. I mean, I'm sure none of us here has read anything quite like your books. They seem to transcend the boundaries of traditional genres."

He pronounced the word, 'jeanreu', making it sound like a Levi Strauss product for French teenagers. McCreadie Jones glared at the back of his head. "No problem, boyo. I've got six bullets. I'd be doing the town a favour. Any more takers?" His hand slid back into the bag and his finger curled around the trigger like a Triffid. He eased back the well-oiled spring.

Copeland smiled those pearly whites and swept that strategic strand of hair off stage to the wings.

"I'm surprised, Mr. Mayor," he said. "With you being a Scot and all, surely you've heard of Andrew McCreadie Jones?"

McCreadie Jones' overactive circuit board shut down as if the national grid had been hit by lightning. The mayor appeared not to recognize the name. He looked to his wife who shrugged.

"Andrew McCreadie Jones is a native of Huntly, just sixty miles from here," Copeland continued. "He is— and I'm assuming and hoping, that I can continue to use the present tense—the greatest exponent of the exotic crime cozy that there's ever been."

There was a loud clunk and everyone turned to see the fat man in the second row bend down to pick up his bag from the floor. Copeland ignored the disturbance.

"In fact," he said, "if it hadn't been for the influence of McCreadie Jones, I wouldn't have started writing at all. I adored his books. Still do in fact. I travel with him in my suitcase. Surely you've heard of him. Can I ask for a show of hands from anyone who knows his books?"

Hands rose slowly, almost with embarrassment around the room. It was like watching a field of barley grow on a time lapse camera. Even assuming some in the audience were putting up their hands merely to impress the American, there was still an impressive show. McCreadie Jones looked around and found himself putting up his own hand.

"There, that's what I thought," Copeland told the interviewer. "You don't forget a writer like Jones. I ate up his books when I was younger. I was as devastated as all his fans when he stopped writing. It's been seventeen years since the classic, *The One Legged Marathon Runner of 12B Wildebeest Crescent*. That was his last and arguably his greatest book. It's every bit as pertinent and endearing today as it was back then. Some of you must have read it."

There were grunts and ahums from the audience.

"Isn't it marvelous?"

"I still read it to my grandkids," called one old lady in a knitted Nepalese beanie.

"And so you should. It's everything real and honest about storytelling. I tell you, I waited. We all waited for his follow up. The next year there was nothing. Nor the next. Nor the next. No word from his publisher. No way to contact him. I confess I'm here on a personal pilgrimage to find the fellow and talk him into coming out of retirement. That's one of the main reasons I came to Aberdeen. I have my train ticket to Huntly Saturday morning. I feel it in my bones that I'll be able to find him there.

"You see? It was because I found myself in this deep empty void without my hero that I started to write. I copied his style shamelessly. How could I not when I'd been so influenced by him for ten years of my life? My books were, I guess, a plea for Andrew to come back. I didn't expect them to sell. I sure as hell didn't think I'd become a celebrity on the strength of what I wrote. It irks the bejabers out of me that they call me the king of the genre. He'll always be the king. I set up the Andrew McCreadie Jones Society to analyze his work. It's big on the net. I state quite emphatically on that site that I owe everything to McCreadie Jones. I keep hoping the great old man will surf across it one day and send us an email. We have thirty thousand online members around the globe."

Andrew McCreadie Jones sat in the front room of his old terraced house. Mama slept in front of the empty fireplace. In her state of mind she probably imagined it was winter and she was lazing before one of McCreadie Jones' blue-ribbon fires. It was sunny out but the heavy orange curtains were pulled and the house hung on to its wintry draughts as if it were saving them till September. The bell had stopped ringing at last. He'd heard the young fellow call through the letterbox. He'd heard Mrs.—God forsaken—Giles lean over the front garden fence and tell him the old bastard next door had turned to drink and didn't talk to anyone. She hadn't heard him move around for twenty-four hours, she said, so he was probably in prison again, "Or, if we're lucky," she added, "dead as a Dodo." Did she know he was a writer? Hardly. She thought he could barely put a sentence together. The young fellow must have got the wrong address. Lots of McCreadies in Huntly.

There had been a moment of silence before McCreadie Jones heard the spring of the letter box and a light thock on the doormat. The front gate squeaked, Mother Giles front door slammed, and it was all over. Got rid of him. Annoying little bastard. What did he know? Web site? Thirty thousand wankers in pajama bottoms and stained T-shirts with no social skills giving up their credit card number for the privilege of . . . of what? Of analyzing the last words and testaments of a man most of them already believed to be dead? Didn't that just prove you could find people to sign up for any damned-fool project on the World Weird Web?

The unopened bottle of Glenfiddich sat proudly
on the tea-table beside him. He didn't have a taste
for it just now. Too much stress. Perhaps he'd get
to it later. What had the boy said on Wednesday
evening? Had it really been seventeen years? Where
did they all go? Seventeen years and he still hadn't
found any words. Ten diaries. Ten novels. It was as if
he'd closed the back cover of the tenth journal and a
steel shutter had dropped between the world and his
imagination. How difficult could it be? The diaries
had been largely fiction anyway. The thoughts of
people he couldn't understand. All he had to do was
imagine more dialogues, invent more people. Writers
did it all the time.

But it didn't happen. He'd sat at his typewriter
with a small copse-worth of paper at his disposal. His
fingers perched beneath the qwertyuiop meridian
waiting for the good but unfathomable people
of Burundi to come to him. But he felt only the
inspiration of sadness. Only the depressing characters
came. All he could think to write was of the lady
selling yams at the market who was beheaded in a
crowded church. Of the overhead-fan-repairer who
had his knees broken with a club. They came to him
even in daydreams. He'd tried to flush them away
with whisky but the ghosts of all the characters he'd
written moved into his terrace. They took over the
spare room and spent hours in the bathroom. They
caused the windows to jam and bread to turn black
in the toaster.

But, most importantly, they forbade him from telling lies. The agent had called every second day. The publisher sent a young girl with offers of more money. They told him they had deadlines. He told them to boil their heads in a large kettle. There would be no more lies. They rode out the next two years of public performances on the back of his last book. They coaxed, they fawned, they bullied, but no new packs of untruths made it past the house spirits. And first the publisher then the agent deserted their wonder boy. McCreadie Jones was left alone to survive on dwindling royalty cheques and memories of the days when he was the undisputed king of the exotic crime cozy.

It was another hour before McCreadie Jones could summon the enthusiasm to venture into the hall to see what awful souvenir the American had left him. He found the envelope leaning against the front door like an unemployed youth. Without his reading glasses the scrawly handwriting on the front looked like half-hearted suicide attempts on a wrist. His bifocals barely turned them into words.

"My dear Mr. McCreadie Jones. I'm so sorry that we haven't had a chance to talk. I still have so much to learn from you. I wanted to leave you something that might convince you of my love for your work and my respect for you as a writer. I could think of only one thing. I hope you can accept it in the spirit with which I am giving it. With the greatest respect, Cakes."

"I don't expect a lot of respect from a cake, young fellow," McCreadie Jones grumbled, tearing open the envelope with the arm of his reading glasses. Inside was an airline ticket—First Class, South African Airways, open-dated—to Bujumbura.

The One-legged Marathon Runner of 12b Wildebeest Crescent

There was a review for my book, Thirty-three Teeth in one of our great British tabloids to the effect that "Colin Cotterill is trying a bit too hard to be like Alexander McCall Smith". Now, I'm sure Alexander is a nice chap and he writes a jolly good book - but here's the honest truth, until I'd finished the final draft for the second Dr. Siri book, I'D NEVER HEARD OF ALEXANDER MC'CALL SMITH. Scout's honour. You probably find that hard to believe (unless you've never heard of him, either) but until I started to write mysteries, I didn't read them. I'm not a great reader of any fiction. I'm belatedly trying to make up for all my stupid years by cramming in facts. No time for pleasure. I have a brain to fill. And it's notoriously leaky.

I was assured by my publisher that it was a huge compliment to be compared to a good writer, particularly one who's making a fortune. I tried to ooze gratitude, but after the 400th comparison I was resenting the poor man bitterly. So, I decided to kill him. I wanted him dispatched horribly so I began my One-legged story. I had ten grizzly deaths lined up for our Al. All I had to do was get to the end.

But I couldn't do it, just as I knew he wouldn't do it to me. He'd puncture my bicycle and graze my knee. That's what makes us cozies. Soft as Mr Whippy vanilla, the pair of us.

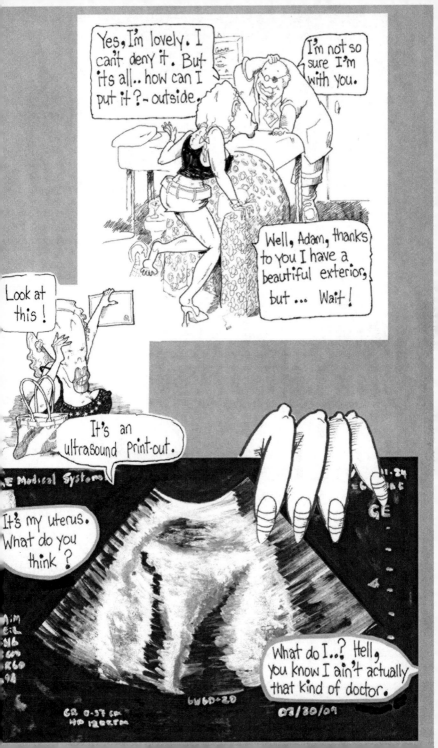

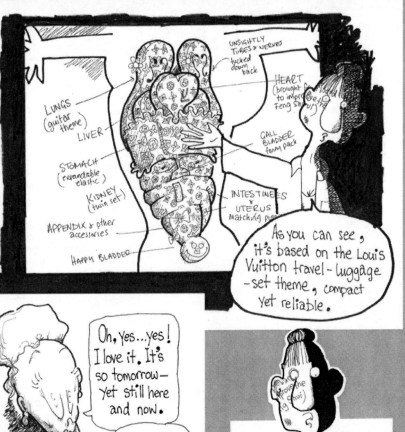

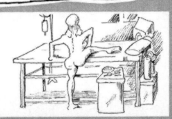

THE FOLLOWING DAY

BUT MRS. WEYMOUTH-SMYTHE-VELAZQUEZ COULDN'T WAIT A FEW WEEKS TO TRY OUT HER NEW INSIDES...

AND SO THE EPIDEMIC OF ORGAN - MAKEOVERS BEGAN...

MADAM DESCROTA BECAME SO RICH AND FAMOUS HE WAS ABLE TO FOREGO HIS CONFUSING FAUX COLOUR-PURPLE/RAP ACCENT THE BIDDIES FOUND SO HIP, AND MARRY HIS OLD PRINCETON SWEET -HEART.

I do!

AND EVERYONE FORGOT MRS. WEYMOUTH-SMYTHE-VELAZQUEZ

...UNTIL

... ONE RAINY NIGHT IN MAY

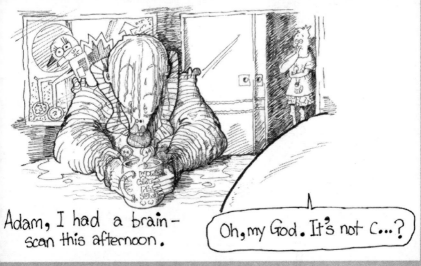

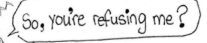

The Inside Job

I don't really have any problems with plastic surgery. If it helps you fit more happily within the framework of your self-esteem then I say, "Go for it". It's your face - rearrange it.

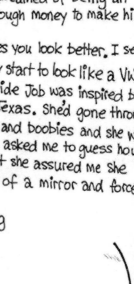

Plastic surgery is just a few pegs up the vanity scale from, say, combing your hair. Nobody tells you not to part your thinni locks on the other side, why should they object if you want to mov your nose two inches to the right? Why did people give Michael Jackson such a hard time? He probably dreamed of being an albino pixie all his life. Then he made enough money to make his dream a reality.

All I insist on is that the surgery makes you look better. I see people so obsessed with "jobs" that they start to look like a VW with ill-matching Lexus spare parts. Inside Job was inspired by a lady I met in an airport in Houston, Texas. She'd gone throu the entire inventory: face, neck, buttocks and boobies and she wa dressed like a flirtatious teenager. She asked me to guess how old she was. I was going to say '90', but she assured me she was 63. I wanted to stand her in front of a mirror and force her to look at herself. She told me she was going to get her eyes widened in a week. I wondered whether they'd be able to broaden her mind during the same procedure.

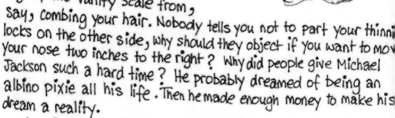

Has Anyone Seen
Mrs. Lightswitch?

"HAS ANYONE SEEN Mrs. Lightswitch?" Siri asked
even though he was alone in the concrete room.
When he opened the freezer door the cold air had
briefly tingled his bushy eyebrows, but within seconds
the draught was consumed by the oppressive heat of
August. The freezer in the Mahosot Hospital morgue
was twenty-four inches wide, seven feet deep, and
a yard high. Its French designer must have had a
kneeling gnu in mind when he put it together because
all that upward space wasn't worth a tin kneecap to a
human corpse. Unfortunately, the People's Democratic Republic of Laos didn't have any gnus, dead or alive.

After the endless drought of that rainless season in
1977 there wasn't much wildlife to be had any more.
They were hungry times. Even the street dogs were
starting to look over their shoulders. The communist
regime wasn't yet two years old but already it had

been able to mismanage the country towards hardship. The three million people who had been too slow to flee across the Mekhong to Thailand had learned to be frugal and resourceful. And perhaps the most resourceful of them all was Dr. Siri Paiboun, the national and only coroner. At seventy-three the snowy-haired little man had mastered every clever subterfuge to squeeze value out of what humble pickings were available.

To maximize the wasted space in the freezer Dr. Siri had created a bamboo litter that formed a shelf and allowed two bodies to occupy the area at the same time. Without it, he could probably have piled four bodies one atop the other like sandbags—five with a bit of a squeeze—but that wasn't a particularly professional approach to forensic science. Siri admitted he wasn't much of a coroner but he did have standards. Keeping his corpses in presentable condition was one of the highest on his list. It wasn't just the act of preserving evidence that led to this respectful relationship. Without a laboratory, modern equipment or up-to-date scientific documentation, there wasn't much to be gleaned from the body anyway. No, Dr. Siri showed the utmost respect to the cadavers that passed through his morgue because he knew their previous owners would be back.

Through no fault of his own, the good doctor hosted the spirit of a thousand-year-old Hmong shaman who had the annoying habit of attracting all the wrong sorts. Every post mortem grievance-holder came knocking on Siri's dreams, leaving clues as to how their lives had been deprived them. One doesn't pile up bodies in a freezer if their spirits are likely to gang up on one for doing so. One takes very good care of them and one certainly doesn't lose them.

"Can you believe it?" said Nurse Dtui walking into the cutting room with a urine sample in one hand and a greasy pork spring roll in the other. She was an imposing young girl whose figure was testament to many such snacks. "We've got a hydroelectric dam down the road pumping out 150 megawatts of electricity but they still manage to treat us to power cuts every other night. I woke up in a pool of sweat at two this morning. I mean the fan's the only thing between me and suffocation in this weather. Did you say something?"

"Yesterday's arrival, Mrs. Lightswitch," Siri said, staring into the empty freezer. "She appears to have fled."

"No. Are you sure?"

"Unless she's shrunk to the size of an ant, I think we can fairly say she's not here, don't you?"

"Then they must have come for her?"

"Who?"

"The relatives. They probably wanted to get her on the pyre before the heat turned her."

"I was the last one out yesterday evening and she was still in here then. Did they break in and abscond with the body in the dead of night?"

"Did you remember to lock the front door?"

"Dementia hasn't set in just yet."

Dtui put her unfinished snack in a kidney bowl and went to stand beside Siri who was waving his arm back and forth in the empty freezer like a magician illustrating how empty his top hat is.

"No signs of a break in when you got here this morning?" she asked.

"Everything was perfectly normal."

"Who else has a key?"

"Only our trusted morgue assistant, and I believe Mr. Geung is still convalescing in Thangon, and Suk, the hospital administrator."

"Aha. Then it has to be him."

"What does?"

"Comrade Suk ran off with Mrs. Lightswitch."

"What would Comrade Suk want with a body?" Siri asked.

"Perhaps her husband pressured him to release it."

"Before the autopsy? The hospital would never have agreed."

"Why did she need an autopsy anyway?"

"Because she was dead?"

"You know what I mean, smarty pants. We only handle suspicious cases from the hospital and government stuff. She wasn't either, was she?"

Siri had disappeared to his waist inside the freezer and was still waving his arm in front of him. His voice emerged like an echo from a mine. "Her husband's a doctor here."

"Really? We've got a Dr. Lightswitch at Mahosot?"

"He uses his first name for obvious reasons, Dr. Bounmee."

"Not the gynecologist?"

"That's him. It appears he insisted on an autopsy."

"What did she die of?"

"The doctor's certificate says respiratory failure under suspicious circumstances. I didn't get a chance to have a good look at her before I left yesterday evening."

"You're sure the porters put her in the freezer and not the mop cupboard? They aren't the sharpest limes on the tree, you know."

"I know. I checked the body before I went home just to make sure they hadn't put her in face down. She was here all right."

Dtui watched the doctor's bottom sway from side to side.

"You're doing something ghostly in there, aren't you?" she said.

"If she'd been removed forcibly there'd be bad spirit in here." He slid out and stood beside the nurse. "But I don't feel anything. It would appear she was happy to go."

Dtui shuddered.

"No matter how many times I'm exposed to your sorcery it still gives me the willies, Doc. What do you think we should do? Write her off as missing in action?"

"Dtui, my love, lest you forget, this is a socialist state. Everything is stamped and signed for in triplicate. If you lose something, you spend the rest of your life being made to pay for it. That includes Comrade Lightswitch."

"All right. Where do we start?"

"Step one, I go to find out whether anyone borrowed the director's key."

"What should I do?"

"You hang around here in case she comes back."

In the People's Democratic Republic of Laos being a director had more to do with who your uncle was than whether you could do your job. Administrator Comrade Suk had been in charge of a battalion of infantry on the Vietnamese border when they called him south to run the hospital. As far as Siri could ascertain, his medical training amounted to a First Aid badge in the Youth Movement. But he delegated well and, to the relief of most, was rarely in his office which was the case on this occasion. Suk's secretary led Siri into the sparse office where six heroes of the revolution hung in a line behind the modest desk imprisoned in their wooden frames. They scowled at Siri. He glared back at them. These were the men who'd stolen his retirement and forced him to run the morgue. Almost fifty years' membership of the Party and they still begrudged him a few years of peace. If he'd just had six tomatoes . . .

The secretary distracted him from his animosity and pointed to the wall cabinet where the spare departmental keys hung on numbered hooks behind the glass doors. They were all there, including number 17, the morgue key and the key to the cabinet was locked in the desk drawer whose own key was in the pocket of Comrade Suk somewhere in the south. He'd been gone since Tuesday and nobody could have taken anything from the cabinet in his absence without breaking the glass, which showed no signs of damage.

Back at his building Siri rechecked the door for evidence of a break in. Its lock was particularly free of scratches and jimmy marks. Few people went to the trouble of breaking into a morgue. Once the door was locked from the outside it was impossible to open from the inside. The only windows in the squat concrete bunker were seven feet off the ground and louvered. All of the louvers were in place, an anomaly in glass-deficient Laos. The Department of Justice had splashed out on an expensive Soviet air-conditioner to be used only during examinations and the authorities didn't want any of that expensive conditioned air getting out. Hence the windows.

Siri and Nurse Dtui sat pondering. Impossible though it seemed, a dead body had been smuggled out of the morgue without anybody seeing or hearing anything. Without any leads as to the 'how' they set their sights on the 'why'.

"It seems to me," Siri said, "that there are two logical reasons why anyone would want to get a corpse out of the morgue in such a hurry. The first, as you rightly said, is when the family wants to have it cremated before the juices start to curdle in the heat. The second—and I'm perhaps being a little overdramatic here—is when they want to avoid an autopsy. To that end, I think I should go to have a word with Dr. Bounmee."

"You think he killed his wife?"

"I know a lot of husbands who would like to."

"But you said he insisted on the autopsy."

"He did. So let's think deviously for a second. Suppose a husband, a doctor at that, kills his wife using some drug he has access to . . ."

"In the gynecology department?"

"I'm conjecturing here."

"Sorry."

"He kills his wife, sends her to the morgue in the evening when he knows we all have to hurry off to tend the cooperative vegetable garden, and insists on an autopsy. He knows full well we wouldn't examine her until the following morning. He then smuggles the body out of the morgue during the night and disposes of it together with whatever evidence it might be carrying."

"Not realizing we probably wouldn't have a clue what she died of even if she'd stayed."

"Obviously not. But he'd be off the hook because we were responsible for the body and he'd shown concern as to her death. And . . . he works in the hospital where he has access to departmental keys. He could have made a copy. He might have been planning this for months. I wonder . . . ?"

"The death certificate?" Dtui took the standard TT567 Medical Practitioner's Certification of Demise form with its two smudged carbon copies from the 'in' tray on her desk and looked at the signature. "Well, what do you know?"

"Her husband signed it."

"He certainly did. What has the world come to when a gynecologist can sign a death certificate? We'll have dentists and beauticians doing it next. Okay, Doc. I'm with you on the husband theory."

"You are?"

"Well, we haven't got anything else to go on. What do I do while you're off interrogating the gynecologist?"

"Can you ferret around the hospital? Chat with those nosey nurse friends of yours and see if anyone has an idea of what type of marriage the Lightswitches had. See if they fought a lot, whether he had a fancy piece on the side. That kind of thing."

"Ooh. Sanctioned tittle-tattle. I love it."

This is probably as good a time as any to explain how a person might have acquired the name 'Lightswitch.' It all came about in 1943 when the Royal Lao Government announced that everyone in the country had to have a surname. Until then, the majority of the population had, like French poodles, been perfectly content with the one name. It irked some folk that they should be encumbered with such a bulky nomenclature just to be perceived as civilized by the western world. In rebellion, some people like the father-in-law of the deceased created silly names for themselves. Electricity was a relatively new arrival in Laos at the time so rebellious Somphet named himself *Sawitfyfah* after seeing an actual light switch in the capital. It was his belief that the government would baulk at such frivolity and force something more conservative upon him. But, no. A month after filling in the form, his new identity card arrived with Lightswitch written in large indelible letters, and from that day on his wife and son and, eventually, the wife of his son would be wired with the same name.

Siri arrived at Dr. Bounmee's residence early in the afternoon. The sun breathed its heat onto the little brick house and wilted the morning glory that clutched desperately at its walls. He walked in through the unlocked gate and stepped cautiously through a minefield of sleeping dogs that lay in the front yard. The front door was closed, unusual for mid-day Vientiane. He called out,

"Sorry. Anyone home?"

There was no reply from the house but one of the dogs growled and farted in its sleep.

"Hello?" he tried again.

He was about to leave when the door opened a fraction and one eye framed in wrinkles looked out through the gap.

"Yes, what?" came a voice.

Siri walked up onto the first step and said, "Sorry. I'm Dr. Siri Paiboun from Mahosot. I'm looking for Dr. Bounmee."

The door opened wider to show more wrinkles and the rather sad face of an elderly woman. She was simply dressed in a T-shirt and an old weather-worn *pasin* skirt. Her hair was tied back with a rubber band. In her hand she held a duster of fine partridge feathers.

"The master's gone, doctor," she said. "He spends all his time at the hospital." Her voice was as tired as an old wash rag.

"Sorry, auntie. They told me he'd worked last night and come home for breakfast."

"He never comes home in the daytime. I don't know where he goes."

"How long have you worked for him?"

"More years than I can count."

"So you know the doctor quite well."

"Know him? Me? I just clean the house, do all the dirty work," she said. "I've got a key. I'm supposed to be here. You can check if you don't believe me."

"No," Siri laughed. "I'm quite certain you're who you say you are. I was just wondering where the doctor might have gone if he didn't come here." She shrugged. "His bags and belongings are all where they should be?"

"What do you mean?"

"He hasn't gone on a journey somewhere?"

"He wouldn't tell me his plans, would he? I'm just the servant, here."

"He doesn't treat you well?"

She looked into Siri's eerie green eyes as if deciding whether to tell him a secret.

"I'm fed well enough," she said.

"How did you get along with Mrs. Lightswitch?"

The corners of her mouth turned up briefly—more of a crack than a smile. "Mrs. Lightswitch won't be suffering any more," she said.

"You think she suffered?"

"I have to go," she said, and slammed the door.

That night, Siri went to sleep with a heavy heart. He'd never lost a body before. He'd spent the afternoon following up on leads and acting a lot more like a policeman than a coroner. But he had no qualms about playing Inspector Maigret. Why not? When you're an old fellow with an attitude you can convince people you're almost anything without actually telling them so. But he'd come up with no leads as to where Dr. Bounmee might have fled. Dtui's research had been no less frustrating. Nobody could recall ever having seen the wife. She never attended hospital functions and he didn't mention her at work. It was as if she didn't exist. Dtui had also done a tour of the local temples but none of them had received an urgent request for a cremation.

Siri's dream that night was no more helpful. He was often visited by the spirits of those who had passed through the morgue. He'd been hoping Mrs. Lightswitch might stop by and tell him where she'd been removed to but she didn't show up at all. Instead he had to sleep through a thoroughly confusing fable about an elephant. The animal went to sleep and Siri could see its dream within his own. It was a ferocious beast in the dream. Its trunk was a weapon that thrashed its enemy, and a tool that ripped trees from the ground. It boasted of its magnificent trunk to the other elephants and they bowed before him. But then the elephant awoke to find that in real life his trunk and his tail had changed places. With a tail between his eyes and a trunk he could sit on, wherever he went he was mocked and ridiculed.

Siri awoke as confused as he normally did. Half of his dreams meant nothing at all. The other half were deeply significant to cases he was working on. Unfortunately he had no idea which were which. Even the significant ones were so cryptic the case was often long behind him when he finally worked them out.

Siri and Dtui sat at their respective desks without an original idea between them. He told her about his dream but her only thought was that he should stop eating garlic before bed.

"Isn't it about now that you say, 'I think we're overlooking something obvious'?" Dtui said.

"I think we're overlooking something obvious," said Siri obligingly. "But it's more likely we don't have all the pieces yet. What had Bounmee's maid been too afraid to tell me? Why has nobody ever met Mrs. Lightswitch? And how did Bounmee manage to be conveniently around to sign her death certificate?"

"And how could he be so calm as to work night duty so soon after his wife died?"

"Excellent point. The good doctor certainly has a lot of questions to answer if only we could find him. We can't even get the police to look for him. No, let's focus on the wife for a second. What is it we don't know about her?"

"Apart from where she is?"

"Yes, apart from that."

"We don't know where they found the body."

"That's true, we don't. We don't know where she was coming from or going to the day she died. That might help. I wonder whether the porters brought any artifacts in with the body. There might be something in her bag. Did they say anything to you?"

"Who?"

"The porters."

"When?"

"Nurse Dtui, you really will have to stop sniffing the ether during your lunch break. I'm asking whether the porters mentioned a bag or anything being found with the body."

"Well, how should I know?"

"You checked her in."

"I did not. You did."

"I certainly did not. Wait! Are you saying you weren't here when they brought in the body?"

"I didn't know anything about it till you told me she was gone this morning. I assumed you'd signed for her while I was over with the filing clerk. How did you get the certificate?"

"It was here on my desk when I came back from the toilet. I assumed you'd put it here."

"Nope."

"We most certainly didn't have an official delivery if nobody signed for the body. Those bureaucrats would sooner take the corpse home with them than leave it here without a signature."

"So somebody smuggled it in?"

"We'd have to assume so. This gets more and more peculiar."

When Mr. Geung the morgue assistant walked into the office he saw two extremely blank colleagues sitting at their desks.

"H-h-hello, Comrade Doctor Siri a-a-and Comrade N-n-nurse Dtui," he said with a big assorted-tooth smile on his face. He was a sturdy, greasy-haired man in his forties who wore his Down Syndrome elegantly. He had been the morgue assistant since long before Siri or Dtui arrived there and they greeted his return with hugs and great relief. Once they'd established that his dengue fever was behind him and that he was fit and ready to resume his duties, they sat him down at his own little desk and began to share their mystery with him.

Once it was told they asked him if he had a logical explanation for it all. He put his fist against his forehead and considered for a moment. Of course, having Down Syndrome he didn't have a logical explanation for anything but he did have a story of his own to tell.

It was a story which sparked a thought in Dr. Siri's mind, a thought that led to one of those, 'How could I be so stupid?' moments. The 'How could I be so stupid?' moment led to a confrontation, which led to the discovery of a body and the arrest of a perpetrator—but not necessarily the body or the perpetrator that Dr. Siri and Nurse Dtui had anticipated.

The Story

Mr. Geung had cancelled his trip home. He figured that if he wasn't well enough to work he wasn't well enough to convalesce. He hadn't quite grasped the concept. At sunrise the previous day he'd been building up his strength by walking briskly around the hospital grounds. He'd arrived at the rear of the morgue to find all of the louvers from the cutting room embedded in the soft, freshly hoed dirt of the garden below it. As he was responsible for the upkeep of the morgue he'd gone to the maintenance shed, dragged back a ladder and replaced the glass pane by pane, giving each a good polishing beforehand. Luckily they were all accounted for and undamaged.

The Thought

Dr. Siri considered this fact. Somebody had apparently broken into the morgue by removing the louvers. They had pilfered the corpse from the freezer and, being unable to exit through the locked front door, had manhandled the dead weight of a body back out through the narrow window high in the wall. All this was done without breaking any of the louvers that lay on the ground outside. A momentous task. Impossible to imagine, unless . . .

The 'How Could I Have Been So Stupid?' Moment

Dr. Siri slapped himself on the forehead.

"Come on," he said.

"Where are we going?" Dtui asked, hurrying after the little man as he rushed out of the morgue and across the crunchy brown grass.

"To the records department for a copy of Bounmee's contract," he said. "Then a brief stop at the state electricity commission."

The Confrontation

Siri, Dtui, and the captain from the temporary police headquarters on Sethathirat Road arrived at Dr. Bounmee's house a little before eleven. The yard dogs growled and howled behind the unlocked front gate but not because they were protecting the house. Once Siri pushed open the gate they all fled through the gap.

"What on earth are they running from?" Dtui asked.

Siri looked around the yard at the holes dug in the dry flower beds and the vines ripped from the walls.

"They're hungry," Siri said. "I'd guess nobody's been feeding them."

The visitors walked to the front door and were met by the unmistakable scent of death. The police captain with a handkerchief covering his mouth and nose boldly followed the others in through the unlocked front door. The stench led them to the kitchen where they found the body hunched over the dining table with its face submerged in a bowl of half-eaten rice porridge. A large meat knife was buried deep between the shoulder blades. It was the last breakfast Dr.

Bounmee would ever have. He still wore his white hospital shirt although the blood had soaked through it to leave only the collar starched and pristine white. From the state of the corpse, Siri estimated he'd been dead for some twenty-four hours.

Dtui looked at Siri, "So, he was already dead . . ."

". . . when I came by yesterday? So it would seem," Siri confirmed. The sound of retching echoed down the hallway. The policeman had retreated to the front porch leaving the pair alone with the corpse.

"So, she could be anywhere by now."

"She could be," Siri agreed. "But I doubt she'll have gone far."

He went to the door that led off the kitchen area, the usual location for a maid's room in colonial homes such as these. He tapped lightly on the door and turned the handle.

"Are you sure it's safe to go in there?" Dtui asked.

"Oh, I doubt she has any more anger to vent. She's done her deed."

He pushed open the door to the small room and there before them was the old lady lying stiff on the single bed. Her arms were crossed on her chest and her tired eyes stared at the unmoving fan on the ceiling. Siri crossed to sit at the end of the bed and Dtui filled the doorway.

"It's over, auntie," Siri said. "No more suffering."

The woman slowly tilted her head in the doctor's direction as if she'd only just noticed his presence.

"Hello, doctor," she said. "I'm afraid my husband can't see you right now."

"I know, dear. I know."

Dr. Siri, and Comrade Civilai, his only ally on the Lao Politburo, were sitting on a log beside the Mekhong working their way through a couple of baguettes that could have been fresher. They were hard work for two fellows long in the tooth. Civilai's baguette was four inches shorter than his friend's because Siri had done all the talking so far.

"So," Civilai said at last, "Attempted suicide by freezer. I bet you haven't seen that too often in your career. She sounds like a real fruitcake to me."

"That's very sensitive of you."

"Well, excuse me for stating the obvious. I don't know too many normal women who spend the night in a freezer then go home and knife their husbands to death."

"She was disturbed, no doubt about that, and terribly depressed. Her husband had treated her like a hired help. He was ashamed of her, hardly let her out of the house. It finally sent her over the edge but she had to have some of her wits about her to conceive such a devious plan. She wanted her husband to suffer, perhaps ruin his career if she could, but she wasn't courageous enough to be around to see it go down in flames. He kept death certificates with his papers. She took one and forged his signature—signed her own death warrant you might say. I checked his real signature on his hospital contract. She wasn't much of a forger."

"And she just waltzed into the morgue and climbed into the freezer?"

"She must have been outside waiting for her chance. Dtui left and I went for a pee and she just snuck in."

"And if everything had gone according to plan she would have been dead by morning and they would have blamed her husband. It almost worked."

"It was very clever. She had a note on her that said 'In the case of my unexplained death, please let it be known that my husband is trying to kill me. I have proof.' She took a handful of sleeping pills, jacked up the temperature control in the freezer and waited for it all to be over."

"Couldn't she have thought of something more dramatic?"

"This was perfect, peaceful and non-violent. I imagine she didn't want to suffer any more than she already had. She would have had us all fooled if it hadn't been for the power cut. Fate begrudged her the dignity of death. The power company said the electricity was off for three hours. She would have woken up when the effect of the pills wore off and realized her plan had failed. She had no choice but to climb out of the window."

"What made you realize the morgue had been broken out of rather than into?" Civilai handed Siri his flask of berry juice to help wash the bread down. Someone on the Thai side of the river was killing a pig.

"The louvers," Siri said. "None of them was broken. It's almost impossible to break in through a locked louver window without cracking one of the panes first. She must have stood on the gurney, dropped the louvers into the garden, and climbed down after them."

"Ah, the wisdom of a man who has perfected the art of break and entry. What do you think turned her from suicide victim to murderess?"

"Who can say? The frustration? All those years of built up hatred for a man who showed her no respect? I wouldn't be surprised if Bounmee hadn't even noticed she was missing. He just turned up from his late shift and ordered his breakfast as usual. I imagine by that stage she felt she had nothing to lose."

"Why didn't you recognize her the first time you went to the house?"

"I'd never actually got a good look at her face. No need for a light bulb in the freezer. I just saw her feet sticking out and left her in there."

With the stodgy lunch inside them the two men found themselves shoeless and paddling in the cooling water of the slow moving Mekhong.

"You know, little brother," Civilai said. "I think this may have been the first case you've managed to solve without the aid of your spooky friends."

"Well, tell the truth I did get a little help. But I didn't really understand it until it was all over. Dtui pointed it out to me."

"You should give that girl a raise."

"I'm surprised at you, comrade. Didn't they teach you in Hanoi that money is not a motivating factor in a socialist state?"

"I must have missed that class. Meanwhile . . . ?"

"She reminded me of that old Lao saying about married couples being the front and back legs of an elephant. Naturally, the woman is always supposed to be the hind quarters."

"Naturally."

"It seems Mrs. Lightswitch got tired of wagging her tail. There's a moral there, old brother."

"Enlighten me."

"If you don't want to end up face down in a bowl of rice porridge with a knife sticking out of your back —you be nice to your wife."

Has Anyone Seen Mrs. Lightswitch?

And, here he is, the man who took only four years to make me an overnight success; Dr. Siri Paiboun. Siri is the protagonist in a series of books that I wrote, set in the Peoples Democratic Republic of Laos in the mid 70s. He's a reluctant coroner, communist and spirit host and he's made a bunch of friends around the world since he first arrived, in relative silence, in 2004. Since then, he's been shortlisted for a Barry, won the Dilys, was awarded the SNCF Best Crime Novel prize (for which I was allowed a year's free travel on French railways, hm) and, the pinnacle of his career, was shortlisted for a CWA Dagger in 2008. Incredible for a 73 year old from a small country most people couldn't point out on a map.

Back in the 80s, I'd become friendly with Lao families who'd fled the communists. In 1990, I went to work in Laos and stayed there for four years. By then, I'd collected stories from both sides of the political fence. I have some close friends both in and outside the country and I return regularly to monitor projects (www.colincotterill.com). I hope my affection for the country and its people comes across in all my Dr. Siri stories.

This story was commissioned by the nice people at Busted Flush Press in Texas and appeared in their anthology of geezer noir, Damn Near Dead (ISBN 10 0976718759) It was my first short.

Fanta Man

HE WAS IRREVERSIBLY old. That's all there was to it. He was old and indifferent and incurably cynical. He was in the wrong place and the wrong profession, certainly in the wrong body and probably in somebody else's life altogether, somebody who'd been wandering around aimlessly for sixty-six years searching for the life that Nimit had been saddled with. A mix up at the hospital. An identical twin mistakenly thrown out with the placentas. A toddler playing behind the house kidnapped by Burmese day labourers. He often wondered what his misplaced life comprised of. All he could be sure of was that it had nothing to do with journalism, probably didn't involve writing at all. If he didn't see another computer keyboard before he died he'd not be in the least sorry. Every story he filed made him angrier than the one before it. Every word they changed, those slimy editors, every fact they altered, every downright lie they inserted just made him spit blood. It wasn't a wonder he didn't have any energy. A man who'd spat blood for over forty years probably didn't have a lot left.

Nimit sat on the sawn-off coconut stump stool beneath one of three Nok Air parasols, sipping a red Fanta. The tall palms that edged the sand had no sea breeze to fan their branches. They hung limp and thirsty. The circus of the day was being acted out down on the beach beneath an assortment of borrowed umbrellas. He'd seen it all before. The cocky local police take the accused back to the scene of the crime. They give him a plastic gun or a blunt bamboo knife so he can re-enact his murder for the entertainment of a couple of dozen reporters and cameramen. The hacks collect their photo and a few words of remorse and hurry back to meet the evening deadline.

On occasions you'd see the relatives and friends of the victim turn up to get in a few kicks and punches at the suspect. The police would stand back long enough for the cameras to record the assault then step in to save the poor blighter's life. But there were no relatives here on Mai Khao beach today. They were on the other side of the world in Sweden mourning the loss of their daughter. Who'd have thought it? They take their girl to the airport for her summer vacation in Thailand. They kiss her. Wish her a good trip. Tell her to bring back something ethnic for the back bedroom. And she's gone. Gone from their lives. Gone from everybody's life.

"Not enjoying the show, uncle?"

Nimit turned back to the soft drink stall where the seller sat in the shade of a grass-roofed hut. The bamboo beams were festooned with fading yellow Singha Beer flags. The man was in his forties. Overweight but he probably didn't think so. Greased-back hair and a sad little pencil moustache that wasn't quite even. Flowery shirt open to the navel with a Buddha amulet the size of a pack of cigarettes dangling at his chest. Soccer shorts. Mr. Fashion. Nimit decided the man had tried and failed at a number of enterprises in his worthless life before ending up here, a raspberry Fanta entrepreneur. No mix up at the hospital with this one.

"I'm not impressed," Nimit told him.

"Why not?"

"He didn't do it."

"Eh?" The man wiped his sweaty face with a cloth and came to sit opposite Nimit. "He confessed, didn't he?"

"I've seen a lot of confessions that didn't have anything to do with the crime."

"Why would anyone own up to a murder he didn't do?"

"Any number of reasons, loneliness, madness, a need for a little bit of attention."

"You're joking."

"Look at him over there, swinging his wooden knife around like Zorro. He's loving every minute of it. Cameras flashing. Questions from the Channel Five anchor. His picture in every paper in the country. Whatever it takes for a few days of fame. I've been covering murder cases since the seventies. I think I can tell the difference between a cold-blooded murderer and a media freak."

"But I've seen him around," the soft drink man was using the cloth to wipe the sweat from his armpits. "Perving on tourist ladies. Trying to chat them up. Watching them sunbathing. Kind of creepy, I told the cops."

"Oh, I don't doubt for a second he's a sleaze-bucket. I could tell that as soon as he started describing his conquests. 'She led me on. She said she wanted us to go back to her room.' Gratuitous details. Give me a break. Look at him. He couldn't get a street dog back to a motel without Novocain."

"Gee!"

The seller seemed somehow taken aback by this revelation. He went to the stall, picked up a glass and dug a plastic scoop into the ice chest. He filled the glass with cloudy ice and brought it over to Nimit.

"Here, Uncle," he said. "Your drink's probably warm by now."

"Yeah, I'm odd like that," Nimit told him, leaving the glass on the coconut table. "I tend to prefer my fizzies warm." He noticed things, did Nimit, things that other men probably missed. He noticed, for example, that the cloth the man used to wipe the glasses was the same one that now hung around his neck damp from its trip inside his shirt. The man returned to his perch beside him.

"All those years. Man! You would of seen a lot, then."

"More than I ever needed to. More than any sinner deserves to see."

"So, then." It seemed somehow uncomfortable for the vendor to ask. "Do you think . . . do you think this was a serial killing?"

"I don't see why not. Three attractive Western women. Throats cut. Beaches in a six-kilometer radius. All in the space of a year. Nobody sees anything. Same M.O. You don't need forty years journalism experience to make a guess at that one. All I know is it wasn't Juk the Ripper over there that did it."

"So, you think he's smart then? I mean the real killer. Getting away with it three times and all."

"Brother, you don't use words like smart with nut cases like this. Lucky is what he is. Look at this place. Even at nine in the morning there are people around. Cars traveling back and forth on the access road to the Marriot. Joggers. Beach combers. It beats me that nobody saw anything suspicious. I know these girls like to get away from the crowds, walk way up to the end of the beach to do their sunbathing where they think they won't be disturbed."

"Some of them take it all off."

"What?"

"Their clothes. Some of them."

"I'm sure they do."

"Asking for it, they are."

Nimit paused.

"And getting it," he said.

The seller laughed as if they'd just shared a joke. Nimit hadn't intended it as one. He noticed the fat man's cheeks redden and the smile linger on his face as he stared out at the turquoise ocean. The newsman was about to push, ask the Fanta man what he'd been doing at the time of the last murder, but they were interrupted. Two of the freelance cameramen had trudged across the powdery beach in their running shoes and were emptying out the sand.

"Got any cold beer in there, brother?" one of them asked the seller.

"More than you could drink in a month," the man replied and hurried to the ice chest.

"I doubt that very much, brother. You obviously haven't seen a cameraman drink." He laughed and nodded at Nimit and took up a place beneath the second parasol.

"Almost done, are they?" the journalist asked.

"Done to death, Mit. Done to death."

The second cameraman was flapping his socks in the still air. "Our friend Juk is currently over there going into great detail about his night of forceful passion on the sand with victim number two," he said. "The hacks from *Khao Sot* and *Aatchayakam* are lapping it up. It's just the kind of thing their readers get off on."

"The only forceful passion that boy's ever had is with his right fist," said his friend.

"The coroner said none of the girls was sexually assaulted," Nimit reminded them.

"Doesn't surprise me. He probably can't get it up," said the first cameraman.

The sun climbed into the vast blue sky and the parasol plastic dried and puckered like the skin on a mangy dog. The whole coastline seemed to be holding its hot breath in suspense. Mai Khao was the last of the unspoiled beaches on Phuket Island currently undergoing despoilment. Developers were bending rules and twisting them into all kinds of shapes to sell off the national park land and take advantage of the building boom. Mai Khao was the airport beach. You could lay back on your deckchair and watch a hundred flights a day ferrying well-heeled tourists in and out of their dream vacations. The locals still appeared to be in a prolonged state of culture shock, frozen in time with their jaws dropped. Nimit had written about the island back in the days when the road had just been built across the hills joining the western beaches to Phuket Town. He'd titled his story, 'Say goodbye to Nirvana'. The Thai Tourism Authority had killed the feature on its way to press. So many of his early human-interest pieces had ended up mugged and bloody in pre-publication alleyways he'd been forced to travel better-lit paths. Nowadays, he just told it the way they wanted it, accurate and dull and unemotional. It kept his salary coming in and his stomach acids down.

The police had returned to the central Phuket Town station with their captive, and the press and TV crews had abandoned the beach to foreigners intent on roasting themselves alive. Nimit and the photographers had finished two bottles of Chang apiece and, despite the vendor's earlier boasts, he'd run out of beer. He assured them reinforcements would be there in seconds. He'd just called for backup on his cell phone. Nimit rolled his eyes. No-hopers with mobile telephones. Whatever next? But he wasn't there for the beer or the company. He was more interested in prodding at the suspicious Fanta man. Just being around him gave Nimit one of his twinges. The fellow had something hidden and Nimit was intent on digging it out of the sand. He'd been playing his like-minded-pervert routine to see just how fascinated the Fanta man was by all this occidental flesh. Nimit would point to a fine-looking girl in the briefest of bikinis and ask,

"So, what do you think of that?"

The answer was always, "Very nice." But the man's eyes lingered long after the words had left his lips.

A twelve-year-old boy bumped over the kerb on a motorcycle with its attached sidecar. He drove across the sand and pulled up beside the stall. He stayed just long enough for the Fanta man to unload the box then spun the back wheel sending sand in a twenty foot arc before speeding back to the road.

"Business partner? " Nimit asked.

"Nephew. He's on school break."

"So, it's just you running the business?" he asked.

"It's me and my brother, Wat, do most of the retailing. We can't hardly keep up. You wouldn't believe how quiet this place was just a year ago."

The beers were warm so the Fanta man filled three glasses with ice and poured for the desperate cameramen. They were beyond caring about cleanliness. They had to work up a buzz before they could retire to edit their footage. Nimit refused the third glass.

"I'm driving," he said. That didn't mean anything. Phuket was one of the few places in the country where being drunk actually helped to survive the insanity of the traffic. The vendor seemed to be retreating into a shell. He served the drinks but opted to stay in his hut and busy himself with a job that didn't appear urgent. Nimit walked over and sat on the ice chest. "You were saying?"

"Oh, yeah. Before the rush there was only us down here. We grew up just across the way there. It was as quiet as the Muslim graveyard at Kamala in them days. We had a little stall, nothing like as impressive as this. We barely made thirty *baht* a day. Then it all went nuts. Foreigners flying in from all over with more money than sense. Buying up plots of land. Squeezing the regular tourists out to further and further beaches. Until they arrived up here. The local authorities started handing out concession permits like it was spirit money. We got hold of two leases cause my dad was on the council when he was alive. They're in our ma's name. She does the books. We've got this place and one more at Nai Yang."

"Nai Yang? There was a murder there too."

"Yeah."

"Did you see anything suspicious?"

"Here or there?"

"Here."

"No. Like I told the cops, we don't open up till ten. People don't get thirsty till then. They need a couple of hours under the sun."

"Where were you the day of the Nai Yang killing?"

The Fanta man's brow dipped.

"We take it in turns, me and Wat."

"Right, so, where were you on that day?"

"I didn't . . . I mean, I got there late. The police were already there when I arrived."

The vendor was pink and sweating like a steamed lobster.

"And brother Wat?"

"We take it in turns."

"I get it. So, was he here for the Swedish girl's murder?"

"On this beach you mean?"

"That's what I mean."

"No. I was here that day."

"Whoa. Bad luck for you?"

"What do you mean?"

"Well, you know what bastards the police are. You being in the vicinity of two killings. They have limited brainpower. They'd put two and two together . . ."

"It was a . . . a coincidence."

"I know that, and you know it. But once they release that idiot, Juk they'll be going through their notes—assuming they kept any—and some bright spark academy grad will notice that your name comes up on two witness lists."

"Why should that worry me?"

"Just telling you how it'll be."

"Not a problem. Look, sorry. I have to get this done."

The collection of bottle caps didn't seem to Nimit like the kind of task to stop a man having a conversation so he knew he was being dismissed. He recognized a clam when he saw one. He tried a few more questions but got only grunts and, "Don't know" in return. The Fanta man had finished with Nimit but the old fellow had barely started with the Fanta man.

"Could I ask you one last favour?" Nimit smiled, taking out his cell phone.

"What is it?"

"I've been having trouble all day with my ring tone. I'm expecting an important call. I noticed you've got a phone. Could I just ask you to give my cell number a ring and see if it's working?"

"I guess."

"Thanks."

The newspaper didn't exactly go overboard with expenses. Overnight bus. Two-star motel. Motorcycle rental and a daily food allowance so frugal he'd just spent it all on beer. They'd given Nimit two days to write a report on the latest murder. The type of story they expected he could put together in a morning. The police said this. They did that. The hotel staff said this. The Swedish girl said and did that. The suspect said this . . . But the suspect didn't do it. And that was where the problem lay. Thai newspapers were wary of scoops. Going it alone presented a number of problems. What if they broke away from the pack and got it wrong?

Lawsuits. Police rebuttals. Lost face. A reporter had to have a shitload of evidence to convince the editor to climb out on that limb and dangle there. Nimit didn't have any. Just a twinge. You couldn't put a twinge in the bank.

The motel room had looked impressive on the internet site but that was because there hadn't been people in the photos to give any kind of perspective. In order to squeeze sixteen units onto a small plot of land everything was scaled-down to three-quarter size. Nimit lay on the low bed with his bare feet hanging off the end. His laptop—a relic of the days when twenty kilograms was still considered portable—was on his chest. It sent an electric charge through his nipples every time he pressed SHIFT. The TV was on in the next room. Five minutes of ads for every minute of drama. His Thai brothers and sisters were so full of advertising there wasn't any space left for culture. Ha, so much to grumble about, so little time. A forty-centimeter gecko was stuck to the wall above the curtain rail like an ornament. The creatures were normally shy around people but this fellow glared defiantly at Nimit and flaunted its orange-green armour. It was a bad omen. It was a bad room. It was a bad life.

He looked at the empty screen in front of his nose and typed with two fingers, "Juk Prasat did not kill Swedish tourist Helga Willander." Pressing SHIFT brought a smile to his face. He pressed it again. He considered writing, "The Fanta man did it." All his instincts told him so. The vendor was there on the beach every day looking at half-naked foreign girls he'd never be able to seduce in ten million years. He'd been in the same vicinity as two of the murdered women just a few minutes after the killings. If only Nimit had been able to place him at the scene of the first slaying the circumstantial evidence alone would have been enough to nail him. But he'd drawn a blank. Nimit had asked him straight out,

"Where were you at the time of the Nai Thon murder?"

By then the Fanta man's social skills had been worn down by all the questions. He'd smiled defiantly and told Nimit he'd arrived at the Patong branch of the Thai Farmer's Bank when it opened that day. He reeled it off like a man reciting an alibi. The bank opened at 8:30 and it was over twenty kilometers from the scene of the crime. Nimit had used his questionable charm to get the vendor's name and address from the phone company. He'd gone to the bank and talked with one of the tellers. She recognized the name and description straight away. He thought he noticed her cringe as she recalled Fanta man's monthly visits.

"Yes," she said, looking at the photograph they'd taken the day before. Fanta man was in focus in the background behind Nimit. "Last day of each month he's here making a deposit that's hardly worth making. And he usually breaks a few notes into small change and asks questions about buying land and fixed interest deposits of large sums of money. It's all an excuse to hang out in the air-conditioning if you ask me."

"It doesn't sound as if you like him much," Nimit had commented.

"His behaviour is . . . well, it isn't appropriate, that's all. Flirtatious." And then she whispered, "He gives me the creeps."

That was all she'd say but it sealed the deal for the newspaperman. On the off-chance the brothers were identical twins engaged in some homicidal *pas-de-deux*, he'd ridden over to the second franchise for a Coke with Wat. Nimit doubted two brothers on this planet could be any less alike. Wat was tall and skinny as a fishing pole with cheap dentures that were too big for his mouth. He looked like an underfed donkey. The only thing he had in common with his brother was a nervous sweat that broke out as soon as Nimit mentioned the murders. Brother Wat didn't have a lot to say but there was something troubling going on in his head.

With his second typed sentence unfinished, Nimit abandoned the laptop and ducked through the door of his mini-bathroom. He wasn't the tallest man on the planet, 160 centimeters in his flip-flops, but he had to crouch to look at himself in the mirror. What a mess. He probably had a line on his face for every miserable story he'd ever written. And whenever he looked at those age-scars they asked him the same question. "If you hated it that much, why didn't you quit before they broke you down?" And he never had the right answer. Because it was addictive? Because it was all he knew how to do? Because it was one of the few things he was truly good at? All partly true. But the correct reply lay somewhere deep where the words fear and failure lived. He'd seen good journalists forced out of the profession by their morals and end up selling T-shirts in Banglamphu.

He sat on the loose plastic toilet seat to do his business and the gecko in the bedroom took the opportunity of his absence to bellow out its evening lament, "*took-kae, took-kae.*" Back home in the northeast they believed that seven calls from a took-kae heralded great things to come. Eight spelled disaster.

He waited for a ninth.

It didn't come.

"Shit."

He meditated on the Fanta man, the Fanta men if he included donkey brother Wat in the reckoning. There was a serious flaw in his investigation. No matter how much thought he put into it he couldn't come up with a scenario that matched the facts. How did the boys do it? There were no defensive wounds on the corpses. None of the women had put up a fight. There were no traces of drugs that might have been slipped into a bottle of pop. The bodies were found laid out on their towels with their throats cut. The possibility that they'd dozed off and were attacked in their sleep was dispelled by the head of the police forensics department. She'd told the press that the angle and depth of each cut suggested it had been made from behind. Yet there were no bruises to indicate the girls had been held.

Why would a fit young woman—three women—stand calmly on the beach and let their killer walk up behind them like a lover with a string of pearls to hang round their lovely necks? Just the sight of Fanta man or donkey brother Wat approaching along the sand would have sounded alarm bells in the heart of even the most naive Western girl. Yet they yielded without a struggle. Nothing was stolen. None of them was molested. No motive. It didn't make any sense whatsoever. He flushed the toilet and watched water spurt from the cistern like an ornamental fountain. And what in fact did the Fanta brothers have to do with it anyway? He wondered whether he—stupid Nimit—was so desperate for a story that he'd made up a plot and convinced himself it was real. It wouldn't have been the first time.

He had a TV in his room. It was about the size of a cereal box. He didn't need to turn it on because he could hear the set in the room next door perfectly clearly. The Channel Five anchor was talking about suspect Juk. The police were convinced they had their man and would be filing charges in the morning. Perhaps they were right. Perhaps they did have their man. Yet, despite the fact that this evil serial killer was behind bars, the authorities had ordered ten-thousand whistles from the police warehouse to be distributed to single female tourists when they arrived at the airport. It was for the girls' safety, they said. Nimit laughed for the first time that week. Yeah, put a collar and tie on a buffalo and you'd get more common sense out of it than a politician. The thought of the local cops running around like dogs every time they heard a whistle had him chuckling so hard he couldn't unscrew the cap off his Red Bull Extra. Thank the Lord B for laughter. Without a sense of humour in this country he'd have thrown himself in front of an inter-provincial bus long ago.

With this renewed enthusiasm for life Nimit lowered himself onto the Lilliputian bed and folded a blanket on his lap before replacing the computer. He'd had enough pleasure for one day. A naturally pessimistic man like Nimit could make a list as long as the Thai peninsula outlining the failings of an average P.C. Like the times when he'd had a little too much to drink and just managed to press SAVE before tumbling into unconsciousness. He'd awake to find the file gone. No trace. No evidence he'd even written his beautiful article. Consumed by the hungry ghost that lurked in the machine. Even on a good day the beast took exception to his impeccable grammar, undercounted his words, and recalibrated his tabs at will. Nimit and the P.C. had a lot of animosity for one another.

But he had to admit his old laptop did have its good points. It spelled better than he could and he didn't need splashes of liquid paper to cover up his mistakes. And it had a vast memory. It could recall his old thoughts at the press of a button. This was one of a number of things he could no longer do. Wasn't even sure he'd ever had such a button, even when he was young and enthusiastic and spongelike. Now he was able to carry around every story he'd ever written. His entire life repertoire crammed into a space the size of a toenail clipping. He'd hired a college girl on her summer breaks. She'd typed it all up. All the years from the very first article he'd clipped and saved in a shoebox. By the time the word processor made its appearance there had been an entire closet in his mother's house given up to shoeboxes.

After two-and-a-half summers the college girl had completed her task and went on to pregnancy and nonexistence as an over-qualified young housewife. And Nimit had his life works on a hard drive. There was nothing nostalgic about this project. Or perhaps there was but he'd never admit it. What he told his few friends was that he'd be able to use his old stories over and over again. Nobody ever remembered. Editors came and went like herpes and there were new magazines and on-line sites starting their short lives every day. They all paid for well-written stories. And there was no doubt these were well written. He often marveled at his old prose. Wondered where that brilliant young stylist had gone. Wondered when the art had been beaten out of him. When exactly had he fallen out of love with the written word?

He scrolled down the lists for '76, '77. He was certain it had been around then. Some time between the country's fourteenth and fifteenth military coup. He found it under '*June, 77. Say Goodbye to Nirvana—unpublished.*' It was a little fussy. Contaminated perhaps by that strain of moralistic overstatement young writers find it hard to contain. But it was a well-crafted piece.

"You're a talented boy, Nimit," he said and knocked back the last of the syrupy pick-me-up. Red Bull. Short term energy. Long term caffeine addiction and heart failure. He read through the entire article.

One paragraph moved him so much he read it twice. And somewhere before the end of the second reading he had it. It stood out like the mole on his nose. So prominent he hadn't noticed it. He knew exactly what fate had befallen the three European girls. He knew why they were dead and had a very strong twinge as to who had killed them.

HOW I SOLVED THE PHUKET SERIAL MURDERS

Nimit Gertpakdee

At 9 a.m. on the fourth of April, I sat beneath a dark green fir less than a kilometer from the site of the third serial killing on Mai Khao beach. There, the blood of Swedish university student Helga Willander still stained the virgin white sand. I was prepared to wait the whole day, or two or three, because I knew eventually I would meet her killer. I knew it because thirty years earlier I had written the following passage about the changes Phuket could expect once it was discovered by the outside world:

'And how will the locals react to this invasion? How long will it be before the roads in front of their houses are paved and clogged with holiday buses? How long before their children are speaking German and English and Japanese and abandoning their regional dialect? How many years will it take before the hearts of their daughters are won by the lights and music of the bars and massage parlours? What psychological mess will be left of those Thais who are caught

in the riptide of this alien wave? And how much of an assault, West upon East, new upon old, immoral upon moral, can we withstand before our souls explode?'

Both vendors and tourists passed in front of me on that hot morning not seeming to notice my presence. I had only been on the beach for half an hour when an elderly woman walked along the packed sand at the water's edge. She carried a blue plastic basket and had on the type of conical hat Vietnamese peasants wore in the paddies. She was in her sixties but her backbone was straight, her posture proud. She caught sight of me half-hidden in the shadows and headed in my direction.

"Massage, brother?" she asked.

The sun baked the air around us but her smile was cooling. The type of smile that spoke every language on earth. The type of smile you couldn't tell to go away. I invited her to sit and rest beside me in the shade. She put down her basket, removed her hat and sat facing the vast Andaman Sea. Powder was thick on her cheeks. She had a fine face, one that had retained its beauty. Although we had only just met I knew a good deal about her. I knew, for example, that she had been married to a fisherman who'd died at sea. A man on the local council for twenty years. I knew that she had struggled to raise eight children only two of whom remained on the island with her. I knew that she had ignored the offers from rich men, offers that her beauty encouraged. I knew that she had sold her family land to a developer for a hundredth of its value because she was desperate to feed her children. But none of them starved. She raised them well and instilled in them the values she had received from her own parents.

I knew all this because I had spent the previous day interviewing her neighbours. Looking at the civic records. Talking to her sons. I was following my intuition. For several days, like the police, I had been tangled in confusion as to how a murderer might approach the three dead tourists and slit their throats without a struggle. In my mind there was only one solution. The girls had put their trust completely in the hands of their killer. Someone they would never have suspected. Someone like a masseuse. They would roll over when told. Sit up. Lean forward. Raise their heads. Put themselves in the perfect position to have their throats cut. A brief feeling of warmth as the razor slices through their jugular. A spurt of blood. A moment of confusion. And the eternal sleep begins. The masseuse calmly lays the girl back onto her towel, wipes off the blade, and continues along the beach. Who would suspect this cool-smiling old lady? Who would notice anything out of the ordinary?

Now you ask me "Why?" And the answer comes from her own lips. She was not shocked or upset when I confronted her with my theory. She had been told of my snooping. She was not surprised to see me. She did not fall into a fit of pique and go at me with her razor. I had done nothing to her after all. She merely smiled and continued to look out over the sparkling spread of still water.

"They show no respect, brother," she said calmly. "Not to us and not to themselves. Would they lay naked in their own home towns? In the parks? By the roadside? I don't think so. Wouldn't they expect their young men to see them as brazen whores? Advertising themselves like meat. Yet they come over here and treat us like we aren't worthy of their consideration, assume we have no culture of our own, mock us, insult us. You and I are of the same generation, brother. Your mother taught you the difference between right and wrong. Why didn't their mothers do the same? Why didn't their mothers teach them not to go to someone else's house and act shamefully?"

She had waited for somebody to speak out. Surely she was not the only person to suffer this indignity. But the outrage of the village elders and the local councilors was muted, tempered by the tourist dollar, and she was informed that there would be no official complaints. The Tourism Authority wouldn't allow it. And as more and more young girls on the beach exposed themselves to her sons, Wat and the Fanta man, the old lady's offence slowly turned to rage.

There was only one way to make the world aware of her shame. Only one way to teach these girls a lesson. She had expected to be arrested after the first killing and the second. If the police had asked her she would have told them. But they didn't ask. Only her sons suspected that their mother's troubled mind could stretch to cold-blooded murder. But neither had shared their fears.

I took my beautiful assassin to the police station at Thalang and she calmly told the officers what she had done. They didn't believe her, didn't believe me. They had their killer locked up. He had confessed. It wasn't until she produced the cut-throat razor from her basket and demonstrated how she had killed her victims that the shadow of doubt passed across their faces. It would be some time before they took her story seriously. But that was their problem. My role was over. Three murders were solved but the core dilemma, perhaps an even greater crime—the rape of a culture—remains to be addressed.

(Phuket, April, 08)

"Nimit? Yeah, ehr, Gop here. Look, the big boys upstairs told me to take a look at your Phuket piece . . . the killings. Right. Good job with that one, by the way. Look, we've decided not to run with it as it is. I know. I know. That's what I told them. I understand. They just seem to think it's a bit too . . . I don't know, too flowery. Too personal. We got a press release from the Interior Ministry. We'll use that for the bulk of the piece. Of course I'll add mention of your involvement. You can rest assured of that. It was a valuable . . . Nimit? Nimit?"

"Something wrong?"

"He hung up."

"Moody bastard."

The Fanta Man

I lived in Phuket on Thailand's east coast for two years in, what was then, a little muslim town called Kamala. The 'good' road hadn't yet been cut across the mountain from Patong, the sleaze capital, and there was no direct transport. The beaches were empty but for a herd of buffalo and pride of place along the coast road went to the cemetary. It was a sleepy place, and idyllic, and doomed.

Once the four-lane autobahn was finished, so was Kamala. The smart locals took advantage of the building boom, sold land and escaped. But many families had lived there since their ancestors walked on their knuckles. They sat on their front porches watching the bustle of development and the end of their lifestyle. And they didn't dare visit the beach any more. The buffalo had been moved on, but there was still plenty of milk on display.

As I was putting together this collection, a girl tourist was murdered a few miles up the coast from Kamala. She was killed by a man who misinterpreted her skimpy, topless, oiled-up, legs akimbo demeanor as a come on. I didn't hear any "poor girl" comments from the locals.

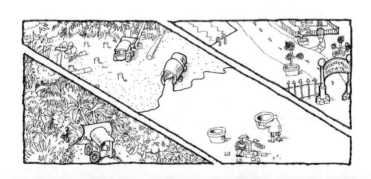

Playing Grand Theft Auto III with Death

"YOU AWAKE?"

"Bits of me are."

"What's that?"

"What d'you think it is?"

"No, not that. That noise."

"TV."

"No. No, it's not."

"Oh, it's the Gameboy."

"Who'd be playing games at three in the morning, Ed?"

"Granddad."

"Your granddad lives with you?"

"Who's Ed?"

"You're not Ed?"

"Eric."

"All right. Close. What's he playing?"

"Grand Theft Auto III."

"Cool, I love that. Who's he playing with?"

"Nobody. It's just him and me live here."

"Well, he's talking to someone."

"Himself probably. His brain's spaghetti. You wanna do it again?"

"Again? We did it already?"

"You don't remember?"

"Tequilas."

"You said I was a god."

"I did? Give us a feel. All right, maybe a demi-god. I need to pee first. Where's your ...?"

"You have to go through the living room. It's the second door on the right ... Oy, aren't you going to put something on? My granddad's in there, you know."

"How old is he?"

"Seventy-two."

"I think I'll be safe, don't you? Give him a bit of a thrill."

"Who's that then?"

"Who?"

"Who? You didn't just see a stark-naked teenaged girl jog through the living room?"

"I was executing innocent bystanders in the parking lot. I've only got one pair of eyes, you know. You sure you didn't imagine her?"

"What would I need to imagine her for? I can walk into any bathroom or public toilet in the country and have a perv. A naked sixteen-year-old just ran through your living room. Trust me."

"Yeah? What was she like?"

"Big arse. Pert orangy tits with upturned nipples. Too much makeup. After-effects of drugs and booze.

I see a lot like that. I'm something of an expert. Is she yours?"

"Yeah, right. I've got a wardrobe full of 'em. She's probably Eric's. The boy's a natural copulater. And, look, will you shut up? I know your little game. Cheating's the only way you're going to beat me at this, fella."

"Yeah, right. Like it wasn't me that invented it in the first place. I take it you haven't read anywhere about my invincibility? Wikipedia perhaps?"

"Then why—oh great cloaked one—did you agree to play me?"

"You. Your big drippy basset hound eyes and your dangly jowls and your whiny voice. 'I heard you like to play GTA' he says. 'How about one last game before you take me?' he says. 'If I get a higher score than you, you let me go,' he says. Huh! Some frigging chance of that, worm fodder. You played on my sympathies."

"You aren't supposed to have any sympathies. You're death."

"I'm misunderstood."

"There, aha! You see that? I'm up a level."

"Congratulations. You're now on a par with the average twelve-year-old."

"You see the shopkeeper's head? Split like a watermelon. Brain fragments everywhere. If only we had stop action."

"And they say I'm obsessed."

"What are you laughing at?"

"You and your desperation."

"What are you . . . ? Shit, missed him. What are you going on about?"

"You and your unnatural desire to keep on keeping on."

"Don't most people want that? Survival?"

"I do get a lot of . . ."

"Ha! See that? Was that quality or what?"

"You're a bloodthirsty brute."

"Thank you."

"I was attempting to say that whereas a good number . . ."

"Ho! Mothersucker! Take that, you scum."

"Whereas a good number of the under-fifties might find themselves playing for time—wishing they'd done this or that in their beleaguered lives—the majority of your type feel a certain relief to be on their way."

"What's my type?"

"Those of you beyond your use-by dates. The soon-to-be crumbling people with nothing to look forward to."

"I've got stuff to look forward to."

"Internet porn?"

"I never . . ."

"Desperately defying gravity DDD-cup Cupid and her Peeping-tom Webcam."

"How . . . ? How'd you know about her?"

"Disgraceful at your age."

"Who told you?"

"You did. Oh, dear. You shouldn't be looking at me, you know? You just missed the opportunity to crack a cop's skull and take his car."

"Shit. I never told you. When did I tell you that?"

"Holy Trinity Church. You really have to be careful what you give away in the confession box, granddaddy."

"You were there?"

"It was me you confessed to. You don't suppose priests have time to listen to all those mundane guilt trips, do you?"

"That was private."

"Don't sulk. You should know death lurks in old churches. It's research."

"You gave me a hundred Hail Mary's, you bastard."

"Cheap at half the price. And watch your manners. Remember who I am."

"Oh, right. Big threat. As if you could do anything worse to me."

"You don't think there can be worse than death?"

"Reality TV."

"How bold you are, laughing in the face of me."

"Bugger it. I've lost my rhythm now. I just missed the chance of massacring an elderly couple in their own home and taking off with their panel van. The machete just slipped out of my hand."

"A bad loser always blames his machete."

"Can I ask you something?"

"As long as it isn't profound."

"Before I go ..."

"There! There, she comes. Tell me you can't see that ripe little melon."

"I'm not looking."

"Of course you're not. Ooh, she's a prime little piece of fruit. Ripe for the plucking. Shouldn't we have just a little taste?"

"No. Not interested."

"Naked as the day she arrived on this unholy earth. Dripping with . . ."

"Who you talking to?"

"Oh, my word. Put some clothes on, girl. Shit! I've missed my drop off. I'm dead. Surrounded by the fuzz. Shit! Shit!"

"That's not very nice language in front of a lady."

"Bugger!"

"What is it?"

"You just lost me the bloody game. And ladies don't strut around a stranger's house in the buff."

"I had to pee. I didn't have time to get formal. Who were you talking to?"

"Never you mind."

"You're a bit nuts, are you?"

"Nuts? I'm more than just nuts. I'm stuffed nuts. Completely stuffed nuts. You flashing your little lemon tarts around just cost me my life."

"Right. Not at all melodramatic."

"I'm serious."

"It's a game."

"You don't get it. I was playing for my life here. Look, would you go put something on?"

"Why?"

"Because you're a little girl and I don't want to be remembered in the local paper as the old geezer they found dead in a flat with a naked ten-year-old."

"I'm eighteen."

"If you were eighteen you'd be at home in your Snoopy pyjamas with your Harry Potter night light hugging your Garfield instead of binge-drinking and Ecstasy-swallowing and randy-teenaged-boy-shagging."

"You a Christian?"

"You don't have to be a Christian to see what's down the bottom of a barrel. I see what I see. You're not even out of your teens and you're a slut already."

"Charming. You got a thing against sluts, have you?"

"What do you think you're doing?"

"Sitting down. You got a problem with that, too?"

"There's somebody . . ."

"What?"

"That seat's taken."

"Doesn't look taken."

"And you can wipe that smile off your face."

"I'm not smiling."

"I'm not talking to you."

"I see. My auntie went a bit like that."

"Like what?"

"Walking around the streets in her dirty knickers, dribbling, talking to herself."

"I'm not talking to myself, damn it. I had a chance. I really had a chance. All I had to do was get up to Level 3 and I was on a roll. He'd never have beaten that. He wouldn't have had any choice but to let me go. . . I can't . . ."

"You crying?"

"No."

"Yes you are."

"It's just hope draining out through my . . . through my eyes."

"This is a bit uncomfortable."

"Nobody asked you to watch."

"Should I do anything?"

"No."

"There, there, everything will work out all right, my little Methuselah ... See? That got a smile."

"Get stuffed."

"Come on, what is it? I won't tell anyone."

"You're too kind. How's this? ... I'm going to die."

"Newsflash."

"No, I mean in under an hour. He'll get his assignment from the underground drugs king and I'm maggot lunch."

"Who's he?"

"Death."

"Cool."

"What, exactly, is cool about it?"

"Are you kidding? Playing GTA III with Death? Man, that rocks."

"Rocks? Where exactly did you learn your English?"

"MTV."

"You're on something, aren't you?"

"Why does your lot have to assume we're on something just because we've got the balls to say what we think?"

"Because your generation usually is on something. You didn't come to this shit hole to spend the night with my deadbeat grandson on the strength of a Pepsi and a ham sandwich."

"Ooh, cruel but true. I was personally in a tequila frenzy. Ended up coming home with skinny arsed Ed instead of the muscle-sack I was focused on. But life's like that. Sometimes you just let it take you. If you're a control freak you never get to see any of this odd stuff."

"Stuff like me, you mean?"

"You're not odd. Just senile."

"I'm not senile."

"Denial."

"I'm seeing everything clear as day."

"Death?"

"He's really there."

"Oh, yeah? Where?"

"You're sitting on him."

"Right. I'm sitting on Death. Shouldn't I be feeling, like . . . a chill? A deathly hard-on beneath my bum?"

"Don't take the piss. He'll have you too."

"You're afraid of him."

"I'm not."

"Yes, you are. You're peeing your adult diaper. So tell me. What's so frightening about him?"

"You'd never understand. You're way down his 'to do' list. I'm at the very top and I haven't . . . I mean . . . I'm not ready."

"Why not?"

"Oh, get back to your zipless sex. You don't give a shit about me."

"Try me."

"Anyone told you how annoying you are?"

"All the time."

"All right. I'm not ready cause I don't understand it yet. I've been here seventy-two years and I don't know why."

"Right. So this is, like, a meaning-of-life freakout."

"Exactly. It's like watching one of those new-age French films where you suffer through it for two hours, get to the end and there's no punch-line. Nothing's explained. Or, if it was you have to watch the whole bloody thing again and see what you missed."

"You want a punch-line?"

"I'd settle for a brief Christmas cracker motto from God or a one-line fortune cookie message from Allah. I don't care where it comes from. I just want a nod that I wasn't here doing a job I didn't much like for forty-five years . . . for nothing. That I didn't waste my time married with a woman who let me have sex once or twice to make a baby then developed a forty-odd-year headache. I want to know that my latter-life porn and Playstation addictions were based on something lasting and worthwhile. That the angels had a plan for me. That there's some pornographic computer game in heaven I've been preparing myself for. I wouldn't even mind if I was someone's lab rabbit. At least there'd be a file on me somewhere. I'd have some purpose."

"Wow! Seriously deep. You want to know what I think?"

"Not particularly."

"I think we're all fish. A bit more complicated, perhaps."

"Perhaps."

"But basically that's all we are. We arrive and screw and make eggs and end up floating on top of the water one morning. All this agonizing and being philosophical just complicates a very simple job. We've evolved to the point of paranoia and become too big for our bowls."

"You reckon?"

"Keep it simple. Nobody asked us to think. Just work your way down mother nature's check list and have a bit of fun on the way."

"That's all there is?"

"Fraid so."

"They teach you this stuff in school?"

"Cartoon Network. Seems to me you're putting in too much effort."

"It only occurred to me when he arrived."

"Death?"

"Yeah."

"He still here?"

"Yes."

"What's he doing?"

"What's he doing?"

"Yeah."

"Right now?"

"Yeah."

"He's got his hands on your tits. He's using your nipples like joy sticks to play his round of GTA III. He's already up a level."

"Radical. You see that? Just the thought of it and my nipples ..."

"You really should put something on, you know."

"You're blushing."

"I am not. You don't think I've seen slightly firm nipples before?"

"Mostly in 2D I'd guess."

"No need to be nasty."

"You want to touch 'em?"

"Don't be disgusting."

"Hey, Ed. Ed! Wake up!"

"Eh?"

"It's me."

"Oh, yeah. Cool. You want to do it?"

"Not now. Bad timing."

"Who's Ed?"

"Look, your granddad ..."

"He's seventy-two."

"I know. You told me."

"Good for seventy-two."

"I know that, too. Except I don't think he's going to make it to seventy-three."

"Eh?"

"I'm pretty sure he's dead."

"Nah. He just looks like that sometimes. Falls asleep and . . ."

"I'm talking—no pulse, no breathing type dead."

"You sure?"

"I guess. Come and have a look."

"Wow! You're naked."

"Don't let that cloud your judgment. Come!"

"Wait! I have to put on my shorts."

"To see a dead person?"

"If it turns out he's just having a nap I don't think he'll appreciate me leaning over him with my cock at half mast. He's odd like that."

"Well, hurry up."

"I'm coming."

"See?"

"Shit! Granddad?"

"Is that dead, or what?"

"Granddad? I don't like the way his eyes are rolled up to the ceiling like that. Granddad? You asleep?"

"You want to poke him or something?"

"Oh, wait. Yuck. I don't think you should see this."

"See what?"

"Nothing."

"See what?"

"His . . . his pajama fly's open. His old-fella's hanging out."

"Gross."

"It looks like he's just ..."

"Oh, don't! Re-pul-sive! Is he dead?"

"He's not breathing."

"So that's like, yes, right? You gonna call someone?"

"I guess . . . Who?"

"I don't know. Some corpse collection service? I can't say I've had much experience disposing of bodies."

"You're shaking. What's wrong?"

"Cold."

"I might have to call the police."

"Why?"

"Why? They might have to send a coroner or something."

"I think you're getting your reality from like, cable. He's seventy-two. He got excited playing GTA III and wanked himself to death. I bet it happens a lot. I wouldn't waste their time."

"Still, I'd better."

"Right. But I'm out of here."

"Why?"

"I'm not a great fan of the fuzz."

"Yeah, okay. That's cool. You know . . . ?"

"What?"

"I don't know. Look at his face. He seems happy he's gone, doesn't he?"

"He's smiling. I think it's like a frozen muscle thing. You seen my panties?"

"Ehr, not really …"

"What have you done with 'em?"

"Nothing."

"You've got a guilty look on your face. Where are they?"

"Can I . . . can I keep 'em?"

"No, you can't. Where'd you put 'em?"

"Nowhere."

"Ed?"

"All right. They're in the bottom drawer."

"Why?"

"I wanted something to remember you by."

"A trophy?"

"Sort of."

"That's sweet."

"So, can I?"

"All right then."

"Cool. They said you're stuck up, but you're all right."

"Thanks."

"You want to do it before you go?"

"That is so inappropriate."

"Really?"

"Ed! Your dead granddad's on the sofa."

"You're right. It's just, I'm . . ."

"I can see."

"It wouldn't take long."

"Shit. All right then. But shut the door."

Playing Grand Theft Auto III with Death

One of the many joys of short-story writing is the fact you have opportunities to experiment. I love cinema and I've worked on a dozen or so screenplays, none of which made it to the silver screen. I've written some rather awful television programmes. The fact that I did all this in Thailand rather than in Hollywood explains why I'm not writing this beside my pool.

I wondered whether I'd be able to write a story that was all dialogue - not a trace of discription, direction or narrative. It would be rather like attempting to understand a D.V.D with the picture off. The challenge was to make the dialogues cred- ible and avoid sentences like; "That's Alan, the Welshman of forty who seduced your mother and stole all her furniture, at the front door." I had to work through a number of permutations before I got it right. At least I think I got it right.

Movie buffs out there would have spotted the shame- less looting from Bergman. I'd wondered how the knight and Death might have haggled in the 21st century without a chess board. Grand Theft Auto III seemed like an appropriate arena. It's one of the many violent games currently numbing our young people to the atrocity of murder. Why not mass- acre a few dozen innocent bystanders before breakfast? I know Death would be a great fan.

It's a dog's Life

IN FOUR SHORT ACTS

ACT 1. 'AREN'T YOU TWO GOING TO EAT THAT SOFA?'

ACT 2. 'EITHER YOU OPEN THIS DOOR AND LET ME OUT OR I'LL KICK THE FRIGGING THING DOWN'.

Ode To a Siam Square Pizza

DAO'S LEFT SHOE stuck in the fibers of the welcome mat as if her high heel was a single stem of Velcro, a Velcroloid, a Velcrasita. Unless a girl could somehow float above that purple rectangle of Astroturf and land on the far side it was impossible to make an elegant entrance to the Siam Commercial Bank building. Dao stumbled, the plastic Geox bag was flung to the floor and security guard Nu bent to retrieve it.

"Careful, now," he said, a warning after the event as useless as his military salute and his unloaded pistol. He held out the bag to her and she threw her hands together in thanks before grabbing it. The silly gift had cursed her already or perhaps it was her own fault. She could have worn flats to work. They didn't actually have a rule against it but they looked matronly, unattractive. Dao had good legs and the heels gave her calves a little extra bit of shape that earned her stares on the sky train. She loved the attention paid to her legs by the white-shirted men on their way to their offices. One day the gaze of one handsome young fellow might leave her calves, travel north past her insignificant bottom, linger briefly on her pleasant neck and come to rest finally on her face.

At night, hers was a chalky Chinese face with features more sketched than molded or mounted. But after a dawn hour at her work bench it became a magnificent thing. In the early glare of the sun she might look a little manufactured, a brightly polished supermarket pomegranate, but beneath the bank fluorescents she was imperfectly natural, almost lovely. She only had to remember to retouch the oils every now and then to maintain the illusion. By the time she'd walked the fifteen minutes from the station to the Siam Square branch of her bank—even at 7:30 a.m.— she was clammy from the irascible Bangkok jellyfish of an atmosphere. Beads of sweat collected like dew on her waxy cheeks. She dabbed at herself with a dainty handkerchief and hurried into the air-conditioned back room, a space where, should you so wish, you could hold an ice cream for the greater part of the day without it melting. The chill slapped her as she entered. In various stages of dressing for the arctic climate were a dozen females, three men, and Gig, who was currently kitted-out as a man but who secretly longed to come to work in a short tight skirt.

"Darling," Gig whispered in his manliest voice. "You bought me shoes."

Dao had no idea what he was talking about until she remembered the plastic bag in her hand.

"Oh," she said. "No . . . It's for me."

"Showing off are you? You want us all to swoon over the fact you've spent half your salary on a pair of Gs?"

Like all of his contemporaries, Gig was a brand junky. Name outranked quality. Logos ruled.

"I don't actually think there are shoes in here," Dao told him. She opened the bag and confirmed that there was a shoebox inside but that it was too light to contain anything significant. She sniffed into the opening. "It could be a severed hand for all I know."

"It's not your bag?" Gig squealed a little too jauntily and looked over his shoulder. The assistant manager had warned him about his eccentric mannerisms.

"This is (as if anybody didn't know) a bank, not a cabaret," she'd told him once.

He dropped two octaves.

"Don't tell me you picked it up off the street."

"Virtually. Uncle Gogo gave it to me."

"You're not serious? Oh, my God. Burn it. Burn it right this minute. I just know it's riddled with AIDS." He flapped his hand back and forth in front of his face as if that might repel an airborne viral attack. Uncle Gogo was an unwanted icon around the Siam Square area, a street bum who took delight in disgusting the well-heeled shoppers. He was too caked in dirt to definitively attach an age to although Dao and Gig placed him somewhere from late forties to infinity. He had a rag of Rastafarian hair hanging in chunks down his back and a skeleton of bones vacuum-packed inside a dark, plasticky hide. His wardrobe hung off him like the aftermath of a dog attack in a Looney Tunes cartoon. It had to be assumed that if he was in possession of anything of value he'd come upon it through dishonest means, which made the prospect of opening the box even more intriguing to Dao and Gig. But the inconvenience of a morning's work postponed their inspection.

At lunchtime they sat in Somtam Now watching the traffic go nowhere in the small lanes of the square. The parking officers blew their whistles enthusiastically and pointed to nothing in particular. Siam Square was a bad-fashion island in a no-fashion capital, twenty blocks of posing. It was a labyrinth of stalls selling clothes that would return to embarrass their owners in photographs five years down the track. Girls from nearby Chulalongkorn University strutted around in tiny black skirts and stiletto heels that made them look like models on a fetish website. Thirteen-year-olds skipped school and went into department store bathrooms to change into the costumes of Japanese *manga* characters. They wandered around the square in soft and fluffy gangs ignoring the rude comments of the motorcycle taxi drivers. In a city without a downtown, Siam Square was really nothing. Through one of those inexplicable quirks of urbanization it had become 'the place'. People went there because people went there.

"He just gave it to you?" Gig asked. Away from the confines of the bank he felt free to replace his funeral neck-tie with a pastel tangerine bandana. He'd barely touched the would-be spicy salad that sat on the plate in front of him. Somtam Now was for being seen in rather than for dining pleasure. Dao and Gig needed to be seen.

"Just walked up to me as bold as you like," Dao said. "I thought he was going to grab hold of me. I backed into a shop doorway but he stood there on the sidewalk and forced the bag into my hands. He told me, 'This is for you. Thank you.' My first nauseous gut reaction was to throw it down and run, but he looked so . . . so pathetic I didn't have the heart to."

"Tell me you haven't been—ooh, I don't know—secretly servicing him behind my back."

"Eughh! Gross. You're ugly, Gig. You know that?"

"Then, what do you suppose inspired this spontaneous act of generosity?"

"I'm surprised he'd want to give me anything considering the way you treat him when we're on the square together."

"Me?"

One of the hip waiters slouched over to the table, half his face hidden behind hair.

"You finished with that?" he asked with a glance at the uneaten meal.

Gig smiled. "Yes, but I'd like to admire it for a few more minutes if you don't mind. Then you can take anything from here you like."

Hip slouched away with no reaction to the come-on. Gig admired the boy's little back end.

"Yes, you," Dao said, putting the Geox bag on her lap. "You can never resist making catty comments when we see him. You can be such a bitch at times."

"Hmm, cats and dogs in the same insult. You really do have to work on your repartee, dearie. And I do recall it's you who hurries us across the road whenever you see him up ahead. That can't be good for his self-esteem."

"Well he smells, doesn't he." Her fingers were sticky from the rice. Only Siam Square could make it fashionable to eat like a peasant. She poured the remains of her ice-water over her hands and dried them on a paper tissue. "You don't suppose he took it personally, do you?"

"Wouldn't you? People fleeing at the sight of you? He's probably traumatized as well as deranged."

"Then this might be a bomb."

She pulled at the ribbon dramatically and Gig squealed. The Charoen Optical girls in their stripy shirts looked around from the next table. Gig threatened them with an eyebrow and they returned to their nattering. Before removing the lid, Dao gave the box a shake. Gig put his fingers in his ears and braced himself for the bang.

"It's light," she told him.

"What?"

"I said, it's light."

"A severed organ."

"It doesn't rattle."

"He's taped it to the bottom of the box. It's probably his own sacrificed manhood."

Dao looked up at him and flapped her synthetic eyelashes.

"More penis fantasies, Gig? You know there's a psychiatrist at Chula who specializes in problems of suppressed homosexuality?"

Gig pursed his lips.

"I do not have fantasies. And I am certainly not suppressing anything thank you, Miss Psycho-nobody."

"You're not? Right! And there I was thinking you were getting married in March . . . to a *woman*. Just how much more suppressing can you be? That's double-shot supresso."

"It's Nok. She's gay, Dao. She doesn't have one female gene in her body."

"I know that. But, as far as the world's concerned you'll be a respectable heterosexual couple."

"Do we have to go into that again? You know we'll both come out of it dripping with jewels and festooned with blank checks and it keeps our homophobic mumsies and dadsies happy. And believe me, there'll be lots, I mean lots of houseguests once we're settled in."

"None that could produce heirs I'd bet. That's the next thing mummy'll be asking for and she'll do DNA testing on it. You and Nok'll have to do the business, papa Gig. Can you handle that?"

"You seem a lot more worried about all this than I am. You're just jealous you can't find yourself a nice gay boy to live with in platonic bliss. Just open the damned box would you?"

"Ooh, so manly."

She opened the damned box. There was indeed something taped to the inside of the lid.

"It's a foreskin," Gig looked away.

"It's a note."

She peeled off the tape and unfolded the paper. A small brass-coloured door key dropped from it and landed on the table. She and Gig exchanged a 'that's weird' glance. The paper was a page torn from a Hello Kitty notepad. The writing was large and deliberate as if a boxer had carved out each letter clumsily with his gloved hand.

"A love-letter." Gig clapped his hands. "How simply . . ."

"Shut up."

Dao read silently and pushed Gig away when he left his seat to read over her shoulder.

"Lizard!" he said and returned to pick at his unwanted peanuts.

"Holy fooj!" Dao said at last.

"I don't want to know. All right, yes, I do."

"Read this!"

"About time."

Gig took the paper and read aloud, "*Dear pretty bank lady. . .* Are you sure this isn't to me?"

"Just read it."

"*Dear pretty bank lady, I hope you remember me. You gave me food one day.* You fed him?"

"Only once. The last two slices of a pizza we ordered when we were doing the auditing. I couldn't finish it. I thought I'd take it home but I didn't want it smelling out the train. One slice had teeth marks in it. I wouldn't call it food exactly."

"Nevertheless, it obviously made an impression. *Not many people are nice to me and I can't forget your kindness. The doctors tell me I must go into hospital tonight and in three days I'll be in Nirvana.* Jesus, what was in that pizza?"

Dao giggled. "You're getting to the 'Oh, wow' part."

"*I once lived what some people call a 'normal' life, but I couldn't cope with the system and all its bullshit. When they first heard about my 'condition' my family bought me a condominium. Of course I never used it. I like the streets better. It's a small studio but it's clean, untouched really. I'm giving it to you. Everything's taken care of, cleaning and bills. This is the least I can do for you. There are so few unselfish people in the world.* Uncle Gogo's giving you a condominium?"

"So it seems."

"For a slice of pizza?"

"It was Seafood Supreme."

"Shit."

"There's an address."

"Soi Kasem San 1. That's just opposite Mah Boon Krong shopping center. It's five minutes from here. Girl, the spirits are on your team. You must have left a whole herd of wooden elephants at the Erawan shrine. You know what this could mean?"

"It was the first thing to come into my head."

"Freedom."

"Freedom."

They high-fived and Dao felt a buzz inside her that tingled all the way to her impractical shoes. She was twenty-two years of age and she still lived at home with a mother she called *the witch* to her friends. The old lady hadn't once taken her finger out of the money spigot; not to allow her only girl to study overseas, not for her to go to university in the north, not to live a life alone. She'd held her prisoner in their unfashionable Chinese/Thai shophouse. Lost amongst the clunky black furniture imported from the homeland. Lost amid four boys, all free and successful now. Lost in her mother's fantasies about what her own life could have been. And to steer her girl on this right path, to keep her what she called, 'safe', she'd not let her out of her sight for more than a day. No locks inside the bedroom door, no gentleman callers at the house, no secrets. Her development had been arrested at thirteen and had remained in custody ever since.

Dao knew what life was supposed to be like. Her classmates at Bangkok University lived that life; parties, boys, sex, drugs, staying out all night, more sex . . . love. Their social lives started at the end of classes, the same time that hers ended. For Dao, moments of pleasure had to be stolen. Lunchtime beers with strong mint chasers. Fondled caresses in the back seat of a car when she was supposed to have been in the library. She wanted a life that wasn't veined with guilt and based on deceit. Was it actually possible now? She'd always imagined she'd have to see out her apprenticeship with the bank and work for a full year to have enough saved to escape the witch's coven, get away from her crone mother's prying eyes. But now . . .

"It's probably a slum," Dao said, although the smile on her face suggested she knew otherwise.

"In this area? Don't make me laugh. Let's go see."

"No time, sweetheart. Commerce beckons."

Dao stood and picked up the key from the table top. The room number was written in tiny numerals and taped to its cloverleaf head. She hurried it into her shirt pocket before Gig could get a look.

Dao stood at the large French window looking out at the concrete sky train viaduct that snaked away through a canyon of odd-shaped buildings. Below, passenger boats churned through the inky black water of the Saen Saep Canal. Her balcony on the thirteenth floor was too high to hear their growl or to smell the rancid fumes rising from the polluted waterway. In the distance, dots of cars hurried across the horizon on the second-stage expressway. New high-rises were being sketched out in scaffold here and there. Lives were being managed and mismanaged at street level and on the flat roofs all around her and she was above it all in her heaven. It was incredible what a little piece of pizza could do for a girl. Everything she'd dreamed of was now possible.

The fat receptionist had told her that all the utility bills were taken care of and a housemaid would come in once a week. In one day, Dao had become the mistress of a studio apartment at the top of the world. It was a long narrow room no more than a meter between the end of the king-sized bed and the wall, but it was tastefully decorated and the smoky mirrors gave the place a feel of something much more spacious. She decided she could get over the unpleasantness of having to look at herself all the time. There were other distractions; a flat-screen TV with a full-package cable connection, a cabinet of DVDs, some of them naughty, a compact stereo CD player, a cocktail cabinet offering every imaginable liquid vice, a small reception area with expensive brushed-leather armchairs and a white-tiled bathroom boasting a natural rain shower and a tub with Jacuzzi spouts.

She fell back onto the bed and laughed and cycled her legs in the air. Her own condominium. She'd left the bank before Gig could get himself re-groomed and organized. She'd almost jogged over the walkways that crisscrossed the chaotic Payathai intersection like vine ladders above a crocodile pit, and was breathless by the time she reached the building—her building. This was her prize and she wanted to claim it alone. She wanted to bask. She didn't want Gig's bitchy comments spoiling her moment. Here was a room to be proud of, to invite young men to, to entertain. No prying mother conducting interviews. No inquisition after every phone call. No nosy maid bursting in without knocking. No damned accountability whatsoever.

Dao threw herself headfirst into her dream life. Her new address emboldened her. She rerouted the few baht she'd put aside for a deposit on a place of her own to the uninterrupted pursuit of fun. She was no more than a fifty-baht meter-taxi ride from any of the serious nighttime venues and she visited them all. She played. She bought clothes that made her feel sexy. She became a clubber, out every night, a constantly flowing stream of Thai and Western men. She drank. She experimented with pills and vials and powders and wore the mornings-after proudly like battle scars. She abandoned Gig early in her liberation and politely made excuses not to attend his farcical wedding ceremony. She decided he was too phony for her. She saw the photo in *Thailand Tatler* a few days later with the Minister of Defense standing alongside the happy couple at the reception. There was some irony in the elder statesman's expression as if he'd seen it all before. As if he could tell that this sham marriage stood as good a chance of survival as any other.

And there were the expressions on the faces of the married couple, Gig with his childhood friend, Nok. They had crossed over their respective lines early in life and remained soul-gays. They really could be happy together because they had never been apart. Nothing had changed in their lives except that they were about to share a name and a luxury mansion and be obscenely wealthy. Nok's parents needed their only daughter married to complete the perfect life-set, an ottoman that complements the three-piece suite. A happily married daughter made the parents easier on the public eye. Gig's father needed the marriage for more esoteric reasons. A gay offspring was a comment on the bloodline. Like son, most certainly like father. In Thai politics there could be no doubts as to a man's masculinity. The union of Gig and Nok was a marriage of convenience for their families and a lark to the happy couple.

Dao wasn't certain why she resented Gig for his lie-based happiness but she started to ignore him at work. Outside, she met old classmates for lunch, girls who claimed to have always been fond of her but had been too busy to get in touch. They planned dinner dates and club nights and soon vanished like candle smoke. Dao seemed to be constantly grasping for a reality she couldn't find. The clubs, the drugs, the boys, it was all part of a dimension based on brightly-flashing, sweet-smelling shadows. At first she was too enthralled by all the wickedness to notice that she wasn't having fun. Living *la vida loca* didn't make it any more *de veras*. Yet still it took her several months to understand why all the merriment was achieving nothing but melancholy.

One morning, while she was applying her bank face in the mirror, working doubly hard on the bruisy shadows around her eyes, she looked at her room reflected in the mirror. She saw it as a movie set with her at center screen. Nothing had changed since she'd arrived that first evening with her overnight bag. The toothbrushes and coffee table magazines and door-front shoes were all hers. Nobody had moved into her life. Like high-rise window cleaners, the men she brought home had swung in her direction for a few moments and as soon as she could see them clearly, and they her, they had moved on to make life temporarily less fuzzy for somebody else. All of the changes she'd been through since escaping the witch had been fleeting and cosmetic.

At last she came to believe that the enjoyment she thought she'd been missing out on as a prisoner in stalag-mother was merely the taste of deprivation. She looked back over her months of decadence and although she would never be able to admit it she didn't actually like the life. And one more thought occurred to her. She'd stepped over the obvious each day and ignored it. There was something far more important than freedom. Something tangible. It was the event that had led to her being given a condominium. She had done something kind and selfless for the first time in her otherwise meaningless life. She had brought happiness to a miserable street person and that generosity had allowed her to learn what a sham the *hi-so* life was. The only thing real in this entire story was an act of human kindness and its reward. With that revelation snuggled warmly in her chest she began to enjoy her studio, not as a launching pad for forays into Bangkok's nightlife, but as a shrine to her kind nature. Her room reminded her of her good self and she spent more and more of her time there. She began to hold Dao in higher esteem.

The building allowed her any level of anonymity she desired. She could ignore people in the lift completely and never learn about them or she could nod and engage them in conversation. In the beginning she'd preferred to be the anonymous mystery woman on the thirteenth floor whose dark life was nobody's business. But she soon felt a need for small bytes of company. She reached a stage where the most valuable socializing of her day occurred within those four plastic laminate walls.

"Actually," she would say, "I was given my room by a starving vagrant who I'd given food to."

She took on a new identity. She gave the impression that she cared about the misfortunes of others. She shook her head sadly for the young mother whose baby was teething. She told the old lady how sorry she was she'd lost her husband. She didn't yet feel the necessary emotions but she was able to conjure them up. It was what kind people did and she was indisputably kind. She started to pass the time of day with the guards and the fat girl at reception. She met other residents in the laundry room and discussed electricity bills and the nearest stalls to buy steamed corn. She liked the play and was good at her role. She was certain the people she met would return to their rooms and tell their loved ones about the kind girl from the thirteenth floor they'd met that day. She wanted to talk to everyone in the building, to spread the news of Dao, the saint of Bangkok. And it was the stench from the Saen Saep canal that finally gave her that opportunity.

Some of the more vocal residents had written their names on a list insisting on a meeting with the building's owners. The fumes from the inky canal had started to affect the health of those living beside it. Something had to be done. The building management committee agreed to meet with the residents on a Saturday morning but few held out any hope. Saen Saep was a polluted waterway that brazenly discharged its pong from one side of old Bangkok to the other. Nobody actual expected the meeting to address such an environmental disaster. It was more of a therapeutic exercise to commiserate with one another and share some home-made sweets. For Dao it was an opportunity to be introduced to those she'd not yet met. Dao, the girl who was given her room in return for an act of kindness. They were delighted to meet her in person.

"Yes, I've heard about you," they said.

But a mystery presented itself at that meeting. Everyone knew that the guests on the first six floors—canal side—had the worst of the problem. None of them could hope to open their balcony doors. They lived in a Toshiba-conditioned world where Bangkok was no more than a large monitor screen at one end of their rooms. But several residents on the thirteenth floor, Dao included, complained that the smell had begun to infiltrate their apartments. Yet nobody from the seventh to the twelfth floor reported any unusual olfactory experiences. The management decided that this had to be a problem totally unrelated to the canal and promised to take a look at the plumbing. Perhaps there was a blockage.

The waste-management engineers were due to visit on Thursday but the stink seemed to double in intensity each day to the point where Dao looked for any excuse to be out of her condominium. She returned to her clubs albeit without the earlier desperation. On the Tuesday after the meeting she was getting ready for ladies night at the Bed Supper Club when she was interrupted by one of the doorbell chimes for which Beethoven had become famous. She'd already sprayed the room with Lovely Bouquet and had four incense sticks burning but the awful smell still pervaded her room. In fact it seemed to be at its strongest when she walked to the door and looked through the peephole. Outside stood a young uniformed police officer with ears like lotus petals and a handkerchief over his nose. Behind him she could barely make out a flurry of activity, people, movement, a flash of metal. She could hear voices and the sound of crying.

She opened the door in time to see an ambulance dolly covered in a plastic sheet being wheeled into the elevator by three men in the uniform of one of Bangkok's gory body-collection services. The now-familiar smell hung thick in the air and the fat girl from reception was spraying air-freshener along the corridor utilizing two cans simultaneously. She sneezed as the mist blew back onto her face. The policeman was looking down at his notebook, apparently awaiting his cue.

"Yes?" said Dao.

"You're Miss Dao?" he asked, still not looking up.

"Yes."

He appeared not to know what to say or do next.

"Who was that?" Dao asked as the elevator doors closed on the body snatchers and their loot.

"Your next-door neighbour," he told her.

Dao was unaware that she had a next door neighbour. Hers was the last room along the hallway, 13H, and she'd never met the resident of 13G. She'd not heard any sounds coming from the room or seen any light around the door. She'd assumed the apartment was empty.

"So that was where the smell was . . . ?"

"He's been dead for quite a while by the looks of him." The young policeman finally looked up and his face was as red as cranberry liqueur.

"Sad," Dao said for want of a better response.

There was another long moment of indecision. She allowed the thought to enter her head that perhaps the man was taken with her and was building up the courage to ask her out.

"I think . . ." he began.

"Yes?"

"I think you'd better come with me."

"Where to?"

"Next door."

"In there? I couldn't."

"We've cleaned up the mess . . . sprayed it with disinfectant. It's not so bad. He died in the bathroom so they could just hose it down."

"Eughh. But, why?"

"Please?"

He stepped back and bowed stiffly. It seemed overly respectful given that she wasn't much older than him. But she obviously had no choice. Her flip-flops sat outside the door but she was wearing her sparkly dance dress so she stepped into her high-heels to complete the outfit. She was about to kick them off at the threshold of 13G when the officer told her she'd better keep them on.

"It's dusty," he said.

In contrast to her own stylishly neat studio, 13G looked as if it was between owners and decorators. There was a fold-up cot in the middle of the room and evidence of fast-food feasts left for the ants and roaches to tidy up. The walls were unpainted and the only furniture was plastic and disposable. It had all the appearances of a temporary hideout for some fleeing felon. To further support this hypothesis there was a cache of expensive-looking electrical equipment; monitors, recorders, computers and cameras all set up on the cardboard boxes they'd been delivered in. A middle-aged police captain was crouched over a box of DVDs in the centre of the room.

The young officer coughed and said, "Miss Dao, sir."

The captain's blush wasn't as obvious as that of his subordinate but it was there nonetheless. He quickly diverted his gaze from her face to her shapely calves and indicated one of the white-plastic beach chairs with his hand. She presumed she had to sit in it, so she did. He returned to his DVDs and she had a chance to take in more of the room. The balcony doors were wide open and the dark-green curtains were tied back to allow a flow of fresh air. "Some hope of that in Bangkok," she thought. Similar heavy green curtains extended all the way along one wall from ceiling to floor. She found that peculiar.

"Miss Dao," the captain began. "Do you know who your neighbour was?"

"No. I've never met him."

"And do you know who the owner of your own apartment is?"

Dao was happy to share her story with a stranger, even one in a uniform.

"I met him once," she said.

"You met him once and he let you stay in his condominium?"

"Yes. I was kind to him and he appreciated what I did for him." The two officers exchanged a glance. "I fed him," she added. "Probably saved his life, temporarily."

"And you haven't had any contact with him since you moved in?"

"I believe he passed away. Giving me his studio was his dying act."

"Is that so?"

"Yes."

"Did you know he also owned this apartment?"

"This . . . ? No, I had no idea. I thought . . . No, I didn't know."

The policeman hooked his finger into the neck of his shirt as if it had suddenly tightened around his neck.

"Look," he said. "I'm afraid there's no easy way to do this." He nodded to the young officer, "Sophon!"

The policeman hesitated before moving to the curtained wall. The drapes hung on rings from a metal rail. He looked back over his shoulder at Dao before pulling open the first two curtains, then the next two, then the next. Dao sat staring into her own apartment as if there were no wall dividing it from this one. The pink rhino on the bed. The bath with her Head and Shoulders dribbling white like liquid latex from the cap. The three Starbucks mugs; Hong Kong, New York and Singapore. She hadn't been to any of those places. Her mouth hung foolishly open.

The smoky mirrors that made her room look so spacious were dishonest windows that left no secrets, none at all. Dao stood. Her legs were suddenly unsteady on her heels. She walked slowly to the thick glass and rested her hand against it. Her towel was crumpled at the foot of the bed. She'd been wearing it when the policeman rang her doorbell. She'd thrown it off and slipped her dress over her head before she answered the door. But as her mind sped backwards over the previous months it seemed pathetically unimportant, almost innocuous, that a strange policeman might have seen her in a bra and panties.

"There were other girls," the captain told her and held up a disk. She looked at him and immediately understood.

"Many?" she asked.

"A couple of dozen, I'd say."

She imagined the men at the police station as they 'reviewed the evidence', making comments about the size of her breasts. Comparing her to the others. Making copies. And that probably wasn't the worst of it. She'd be on the internet by now. They'd be in New Delhi and Birmingham, England watching her perform inexpert fellatio.

"It was a one-man operation by the looks of it," said the captain, obviously uncomfortable with the silence. She stood staring at her TV. She'd left it on. Big Brother Thailand; a bunch of insincere people acting unnaturally because they knew there were cameras on them. Whereas she'd been totally unaware there were cameras yet she'd spent three months pretending anyway. Her every lie to herself was on DVD. Her whole fake self was recorded. The policeman was still mumbling behind her.

"It was all an act," he said. "From the documents and bank-books, it looks like the man was well off. He made himself up as a bum and hung around begging till some unsuspecting young lady such as yourself gave him a few baht or a few kind words. Then he'd go into his 'I have to repay your kindness' routine. It's all documented on one of his websites. He was proud of himself, the old boy."

Dao felt a chill run down her spine. The two policemen and the general public of the cyber world for many years to come would watch her act out her disappointing fantasy life; her crying with disappointment as every adventure fizzled into meaningless soot, her failure to drink or smoke or love with any conviction. They'd see she wasn't fun-loving material. But even that seemed somehow insignificant compared to the shattering of her newly born image. She couldn't even convince herself any more that she was kind. Her act of charity had not been selfless. It was an afterthought, tossing a half-eaten pizza in the direction of a bum to keep him from approaching her. And it got the result it deserved. She was a fake.

The captain held up a wad of bankbooks for her to look at but she was staring with tears in her eyes at the photo on her bedside table. Dao and her mother and the four boys on Hua Hin beach when she was ten. When she was protected. When she was safe from life.

Ode to a Siam Square Pizza

" THE SIMPLE BLACK AND WHITE UNIFORM ERASES ALL SOCIAL AND ECONOMIC BACKGROUND AND MAKES ALL UNIVERSITY STUDENTS OF ONE CLASS- SCHOLARS"
(MINISTRY OF EDUCATION)

I taught University stude
in Thailand for a number of
years: kids from different ba
grounds coming together for 4
years, rich and poor, equally
baffled by the education syste

A lot of the hi-so girls trea
a university like a beauty parlo
one more process towards buil
a complete, marriageable wife.

These Paris Hintons (Thai pronunciation) didn't need to be too e
cated. Just a tweak here, a highlight there. Some already had
their suitors selected at nursery school.

Then there were the "Nouveau Biche": girls on the edge wh
had all the moves and the money but had no hope of getting in to t
inner circle. Wrong name. Wrong background. What happened to th
after graduation? Their futures weren't mapped out by mummy
and daddy.

I wanted to make a snapshot of
one of these aspiring high-socialit
to highlight the disillusionment
that comes with the realization the
been clutching at bubbles, the
confusion of being brought up with
perfectly good culture of their own
and attempting to switch to an
inappropriate, Western one.

I lived in Dao's condominium in Bangkok for a year and ate at
Siam Square surrounded by all those confused youngsters. I
made notes on the back of Pizza Hut fliers. And here, years
later, I have a chance to use them.

MORAL :- Never throw anything away.

Life as a Torreja

8.

THE LITTLE ASIAN guy ambled over to the cashier with a strawberry Slurpee in his right hand and a corn dog in his left. He was barely taller than the chewing gum stand. He put his purchases on the counter and smiled. It was the type of smile that might have been confused with sarcasm if you didn't know him. And nobody really did. He was kind of anonymous. His skin showed no evidence of exposure to the elements, or insects, or abuse or ageing. If he'd held up the store the police artist would start and end with a blank sheet of paper. He was like a specimen who'd been cocooned in tin foil for seventy years and finally released for a trip to the 7-Eleven.

"That all?" The cashier was one of those gangly, unhealthy-looking creatures that made a 7-Eleven uniform look worse than it already did. When they put together their 'one style fits all' retail fashion range, the designers must have figured in pimples. The boy was colour-coordinated, red and black.

"That is the works, thank you very much," said the Asian guy. Once spoken, his voice crumbled like chalk as if the words could never be retraced.

Excessive politeness made the clerk jumpy. He was used to rude. Abrupt and rude. That was the night shift. Abrupt, rude, high and drunk idiots ruled the darkness. Spaced-out junkies. Aliens who landed in the A/C fluorescent universe and were fascinated by everything but didn't have any earth money to make a purchase. Gang members on their way home from a hectic night of drive-by slayings. Street teenagers seeing how many profanities they could squeeze into one sentence. Bag ladies asking what they could get in exchange for a perfectly good right shoe. The clerk knew how to respond to rude and weird. He was one of them. But politeness was too sinister even for him. He glared at the Asian guy and rang up the purchase. Yet, even after he'd received his change the little man stood his ground.

"Something else?" the clerk asked.

The Asian seemed to be struggling with a loose ball bearing between his ears. His head dipped first left then right. Then he smiled again and spoke so softly the sound was almost lost beneath the mechanism of the hotdog rotisserie.

"You will be threatened by a man with a knife," he said. "He is not a violent man, merely down on his luck. If you hand over the one hundred and eighty-two dollars you have in your cash register he will go away. If you put up a fight there will be a scuffle and you will accidentally be stabbed in the stomach. You will die on your way to the hospital."

The youth reached below the counter.

"You threatening me, bro?"

"Goodness me, no. I'm just passing on the message. You are at a crossroads. Your fate is in your hands. I wish you all the very best of luck. Goodnight to you."

With that, he turned and walked to the door and looked up with pleasure as the chime bid its mechanical farewell. The clerk watched him meld into the dark night outside.

"Yeah, right. Like, come again . . . or whatever."

The boy had orders to fill out and a company questionnaire to answer but the cash register tweaked at his curiosity. He rang up No Sale and flipped through the bills in the tray.

"Yeah, wow. Good trick, man. Good trick."

7.

It was two-something on a Wednesday morning. All the righteous, hardworking citizens were in bed or comatose in front of the TV with tortilla chip crumbs down their fronts. There was only one customer in the 7-Eleven. He was a gangly black giraffe of a man. His impressive forehead sloped at a forty-five degree angle to an overhang of unkempt eyebrow hair. His dark features huddled there in its shadow like refugees sheltering from the sun. He'd spent the last ten minutes of his life in the back aisle studying English from Listerine labels. It was a lesson that probably wouldn't stick. The half of his brain he used for language learning was focused on the fact he hadn't eaten since Tuesday morning. He was so numb with hunger he could barely feel the dog bite on his skinny ankle. The blood had dried already on his cuff. He didn't give a thought to the fact he'd probably contract rabies and die. If he survived starvation this morning he could deal with death some other time.

One look at his clothes told you he wasn't from the south side. Not any side of Chicago. There was a clause in the black constitution that stated categorically African Americans were not allowed to wear white nylon button—collar shirts and Staypress slacks—both a size too small. His black lace-ups without socks didn't make it onto the list. The guy wasn't even from this side of the planet. He had a long loping bushman-out-of-his-element walk. He was so Dark Continent the brothers didn't even give him a 'wassup?' on the street. The Roots days were a generation away. In 2008, Africans were aliens.

The hunger rumbled from his stomach and up into his chest like the upstairs neighbours moving a piano. It was time. Hungry men—desperate measures. The knife was tucked in his belt beneath his shirt flaps. He headed toward the cashier's counter. As he passed the dark glasses and discount hat stand he grabbed a Dodgers cap. It was too small for him. He should have tried for a larger one but his adrenaline was pumping too fast to go back. He pulled the peak down over his eyes. To keep it from sliding down his forehead he had to tilt his head back. This defeated the purpose of wearing it. But nothing mattered, except . . .

The electronic chime above the door sounded and a little Asian guy walked in with a sarcastic smile plastered across his face. The African stopped and turned on his heel. He clicked his fingers as if he'd just remembered something and went back to the Listerine shelf.

6.

Like lacrosse, reincarnation has its rules. You don't just choose to come back as Stephen King. "With the three-million bucks advances but without the car accident, thanks." You take what you're given. In Rhonda's case, the choices were limited by the way she'd lived her life. You treat everyone around you like dogs and you come back as a dog. Simple as that. She'd never have thought it could be that clear-cut and permed. Dogs try to tell us. They try to explain they were once the president of the Philippines, or Genghis Khan, or a divorce lawyer, but it just comes out as whimpers and nocturnal barks and mournful stares. It doesn't take too long for them to realize they're basically screwed, and soon, everything levels out to the three fundamentals; somewhere to eat, somewhere to sleep, somewhere to shit.

Some dogs have all three taken care of for them. They're reborn as Shih-tzus, which has its own distinct scent of hell. Pol Pot came back as a Shih-tzu. Can you imagine it? All the petting? The dress-ups? But, considering the alternative, Rhonda would have given her right paw to come back a Shih-tzu or a Pekinese or an anorexic Chihuahua. She hadn't been nearly that lucky. From chief editor of Shoeman and Shaister, the publishers, to street mongrel in under twenty seconds. She didn't even have time to grab a few hors d'oeuvres for the journey. A chicken bone in the throat and not a damned soul around who'd learned the Heimlich maneuver. She was still choking when she slid from the bloody slime of her mother's womb. And so it started. Eight long years in the garbage-strewn alleyways of Chicago with nothing to read and be sarcastic about.

Ah, it wasn't all that bad. It had its moments. Just an hour ago some old tramp lady had given her half a pack of Cheetos. There were magic moments like that. A big fan of Cheetos was Rhonda. She could still taste the stale cheese between her teeth. But food just made her think of food. She lay beneath a wooden bench opposite the all night Burger King and imagined what it would be like to stroll in there and order a Whopper. "Yes, ma'am. Fries with that?" There was a guy in there doing just that. He paid, walked out onto the street, unwrapped a bacon double cheeseburger and started eating it right there on the sidewalk. Rhonda lurched across the road and took up a spot in the shadows close enough to clean up any droppings. The guy took a big juicy bite out of his burger and hailed the only cab on the street. The driver was from Pakistan or some such place. He had a 3D paper popup of Mecca on the passenger dashboard. He refused to let the guy into his cab with a slice of pig in his mitt. You could see the guy chewing the dilemma over. But, as a taxi at 2 a.m. was more precious than supper, he took a last bite and tossed the whole meal into the nearest trash receptacle. He jumped in the cab and they sped off.

Rhonda was alert to this. After eight years in back alleys and thirty-seven kids you get street savvy when it comes to food. There are other hunters out there and a moment of hesitation could mean the difference between filling your belly and passing out from hunger. Hers wasn't a long-legged breed, some might describe her as stunted, and all those tits weighed her down like a lead ballast belt, but somehow she was up on the lip of the bin in seconds looking down at her breakfast. And just as suddenly it was gone from under her. Some claw-fisted basketballer type had reached in there and snatched her burger. Man, she detested those blacks. There wasn't a one of them under fifty could write worth a shit. This young generation was all filth and abuse of grammar. And now here was one of the bastards stealing food from the mouth of a down-and-out dog. No respect.

She dropped from the can and gave chase, snarling yellow saliva through barbed teeth. The tall fella looked back at her but reacted too slowly. She clamped her fangs around his ankle. It took a while for the pain to make its way up his mile-long body to his brain but once it got there his instinct let him down. He screamed and used the burger as a weapon to beat off the mad dog. Rhonda gladly took a bun to the face and watched the slab of meat fly off into the gutter. She let go the bony ankle, scooped up the beef in her jaws and was gone.

5.

Dora owned what her parents would have referred to as a perambulator. There had been a time when nannies in petticoats wheeled it around Lincoln Park with high society babies aboard throwing up chopped liver pâté all over themselves. But, had it contained a hi-so baby this night, that child would have been flat as a disappointment by now. The wagon was piled high with black plastic bags and cardboard boxes and all kinds of memorabilia. Dora's world was upwardly mobile.

There was a misconception in Illinois—perhaps all across the world—that women who wheeled their lives around in supermarket trolleys or old strollers had to be as daft as bats. If they weren't daft they were addicted to something. At the very least they were slaves to the bottle. But Dora wasn't any bottle's slave and *daft* is relative. She was just a free-spirited woman with glandular problems and a mild hatred of human kind. We all have such animosity buried within us to some extent but Dora's aversion to people had burrowed its way to the surface. The only way she could deal with her fellow man was to juxtapose the roles of humans and animals. She would have a deep philosophical discussion with the pigeons then give a policeman a stale corner of biscuit and pat him on the head. It worked for her if not for the cop.

"I feel for you, honey," she said.

The saggy-titted bitch sitting across from Dora's bench looked up with one of those human expressions that fool you into believing there's something logical going on inside their brains.

"Yeah, you know what I'm talking about, sister. You been through the mill. You been treated bad. I can relate, honey. Really I can. They can be cruel, those people. And deceitful. You can take that as gospel. And you know who you gotta be careful of? Them. The secret police. They're everywhere, honey. Just everywhere. I realize to you they'd just look like regular shitty human bein's. But I see 'em. Oh yeah. They hide in the bushes and they grab people. I didn't see 'em grab no dogs as yet but that time'll come. You mark my words. That government of theirs denies it's happening. I went to City Hall and I told 'em and they lied right in my face. Denied, denied, denied. But you can't deny what I seen with my own eyes. What I hear with my own ears."

The dog was looking around uncomfortably like a music lover who'd accidentally stumbled into a karaoke parlour. But Dora walked over to her push chair and started fumbling around. There was hope.

"You know why I think they're grabbing 'em, honey? Cause they're wasteful, that's why. I think they're the wastefulness secret police. I sure hope so. I mean, take a look at this."

Dora unwrapped a plastic bag and the dog's tail started swatting at moths. The lady pulled out a shoe. The dog put her tail at ease and looked around again for hope.

"Pay attention here, girl. Look at this. This ain't no Wal-Mart's ten dollar job. This is a piece of art. Brand new. It must be worth half a million bucks just by itself and I can't even exchange it for a tuna sandwich. Can you believe that? Nobody wants it. And who in their right mind would throw out one pretty shoe? And that ain't all. There's stuff like this."

The dog turned her head in time to see the woman pull a crushed Cheeto Snack packet from the pile.

"I'd hazard a guess this is more up your alley, so to speak. But it's the same old story. Waste. They got zoo animals starvin' to death in Iraq and here we are throwin' out perfectly good nutritious food. I ask you."

She opened the flaps and spent far too long manipulating the packet back into its original box shape. By the time it was evened out there was enough dog drool on the path to float ducks in.

"Would you care to join me for supper? Ha, yeah, I guess you would."

Dora held out a handful of snacks and the dog ambled slowly toward her with her tail flapping up a wind, reluctant to get within slapping distance.

"Yeah, you been beat before, ain't you, honey. Here now. Take your time. There's plenty to go round. They tried to grab me, too, you know? The secret police. Oh, yeah. Two of 'em jumped out at me and asked me where

I was from. I whistled at 'em. It confuses people when you do that. I whistled and I offered 'em pea shucks. But I guess they wasn't hungry. One of 'em asks, 'You got any I.D.?' The other one, some little girly in a fat waistcoat that made her look like a skinny-legged orangutan gorilla, or somethin', she started pokin' through my things. Now, sister, I tell you, I don't let nobody poke through my things. I told her straight. I said, 'Girl, if you touch one more of my things you'll be face down in some ER getting a park bench removed from your ass.' That's what I told her. I thought they might of shot me for that but the guy just laughs and he says, 'That's about as American as you can get,' and they're gone. Just like that. Vanished back into the shadows they come out of. Hey, slow down, honey. You gonna take my finger off if you don't chill out some."

Dora felt down into the depths of the pack and shook out the crumbs.

"Damn, that was almost a full pack you just snorted. See? They all gone. You did good. Still, I guess none of them kids of yours send you nothin' through the mail on bitchin' day. You gotta take what you can get. Am I right? We all gotta take what we can get. We gotta beat this system. Cause if you don't beat them, they're gonna beat you. Oh, I know what you're thinkin'. You're thinkin', 'This woman is paranoid.' And I tell you, honey, I am. I admit it. I'm paranoid. But all these secret police and spies and hidden cameras and shit, they're enough to make anyone paranoid. Am I right, hon? Now where'd you go?"

4.

It was exquisite, so snug it might have been varnished onto Edwin's foot. He was a dainty man, evolved from a delicate teenager and a positively fragile and sickly baby. And his was a ballerina's left foot. And this was the ultimate shoe for it, Bottega Veneta snakeskin, sleek ankle strap and graceful, swanlike heel. A snap at $570. The caviar of left shoes.

It's partner lay on its side in mocking disrespect at the center of the sheepskin rug. It was a wonder how one shoe could be loveable and the other so disagreeable. Edwin felt a surge of anger toward it. But that was fine. His sensibilities mentor had urged him to channel his aggression into inanimate objects. It was acceptable to be angry at, say, a shoe, but not at the rude sales-bitch who sold it to one. Had she never seen a one-legged man buy a pair of women's shoes before? Her jaw had positively crashed to the marble tiles when he sat to try it on. He'd had a good mind to tell her what to do with her footwear but, well, it was such a lovely shoe. Such a treasure.

He owed God a debt of thanks for not making him a transvestite. How did those poor men put up with the gawking lobotomy patients they had working in larger ladies fashion departments? Thank heaven he merely had a penchant for elegant shoes. He had no desire to wear them in public. He hadn't, not even before . . . not even when . . . The anger rose again in his throat.

"Breathe through it, Edwin," he told himself. "Channel."

He picked up a lilac scatter-cushion from the sofa and squeezed all his wrath into it, believed he could hear those little duck feathers inside squealing with pain.

"Breathe through it and forgive, Edwin. Forgive."

Forgive the idiot who'd taken his leg . . . by mistake. Hey, buddy was that your leg? Sorry.

"Breathe, Edwin. Look at the positives."

There were positives. A massive compensation package from the city, a compassionate promotion at work, certainly a good deal more action on the bedsprings, "Wink, wink". It wasn't beyond an ex-pretty fifty-five-year-old gay man to play on the sympathies of young gentlemen. Some of them seemed to view it as community service, sexual favours for the handicapped. Edwin didn't have any trouble living with that. It was certainly no more despicable than luring young things back to his apartment under false pretenses, and hell, how many times had he gotten away with that little ruse?

"I don't know, honey. It's soooo close to publishable it aches. It just needs—I don't know—a little something. A tweak here and there. Look, I know I'm the senior editor (thank you Rhonda for dying horribly and making that possible) and ethically I shouldn't be suggesting this, but it really is so special perhaps I could give you one or two pointers. I have a few hours free (and a bottle of Moet in the refrigerator) on Friday, why don't you come over and . . . ?"

And they came. And some were so desperate to see their names on the spine of their awful books they let him do what he wanted with them because, "Hey, whatever it takes, man." He'd said that, Edwin's protégé of the month. The skinny guy with the pimples. The byte-writing ambassador of two-dimensional pop-culture. The living dead. The boy who thought, 'like, good shit, man' was an adequate turn of phrase to describe everything he'd ever read including the one or two tomes without cartoon illustrations. But with the light out there was something Nureyevesque about him. And fifty-five was the new ninety for gay men. You had to take whatever you could get. It was worth an hour of editorial deception. But the day would come when Edwin had to confess there was more literature on a compressed air tank warning label than in the boy's five-hundred pages. Perhaps he should look seriously into turning his casual convenience store position into something more like a career.

But there was the meantime and Edwin needed the physical release as an outlet for all that anger. There weren't enough scatter cushions on the planet to squeeze that hurt out of him. Better to have sex with a moron than walk into the local precinct house with a loaded Uzi and . . .

"Breathe it out, Edwin. Release the blame. Forgive."

With great reluctance he slid the Veneta from his foot and laid it gently on the sofa. He was too emotionally torn for fetishism. He hopped to the kitchen and pirouetted, hoping that some distraction might call to him. His unbalanced form was reflected in the shiny silver of the refrigerator, a costly monolith paid for by the city. The merest touch opened the door. His

Mexican cleaning woman had left him an *o-bento* from Edo's. It was his favourite Japanese and he knew that unless you ate sushi within three hours of its creation it turned into clay figurines. But he wasn't in the mood for that either. What had promised to be a super shopping day had turned to kaka right in front of his eyes. And it was all down to that darned right shoe.

"Channel. Vent."

In the bedroom he pulled on his baggy cream chinos and took his crutch from its hook. He collected the evil sister shoe from the living room carpet and swore at it as he took it into the hallway. Out of sheer spite he bumped it twice against the metal flap before sending it down the garbage chute. There was no sound. If there was any justice in the world, the vindictive partner of his beloved designer shoe had landed in something slimy and smelly. That would teach it.

3.

They sat on either side of the little Formica table, big, flat-headed, muscle-turned-to-fat. They might have been mistaken for extras in a mob movie. They were way out of scale for a Japanese restaurant. Probably too big for Dennys. The new guy was trying to break apart the wooden chopsticks with his clumsy fingers.

"I don't know," he said.

"What don't you know, Mel"

"This place. I tell you, I haven't eaten since lunchtime yesterday. I need some food."

"It's coming."

"No, I mean restaurant food."

"What do you think this is, a laundry?"

"No, Charlie. In my mind, Japanese is where you take a date when you're not hungry. You nibble at shit and take in the atmosphere then go home and stuff your face with waffles. It's not somewhere you go to pig out. It's not like Chinese, for God's sake, where they fill you up till you can't eat any more then they arrive with the main course. Japanese food is more of a scratch-n'-sniff culinary experience."

"Ah, Mel, this place will change your entire perception. I ordered us the *teshoku*. At Edo's you get man-sized sushi and bottomless *miso*. They bring you all the rice you can eat."

"Same effect as filling yourself up with polystyrene bubbles, I'm told."

The old-timer laughed and snapped apart his chopsticks loudly with one hand. The counter patrons all looked over their shoulders at the same time like synchronized swimmers before returning to their comics and noodles.

"Now, there's the attitude we've all come to love and respect from our law enforcement officers."

"I'm with Immigration, pal."

"Right. I forgot. Me too."

"So far I've had a week of rumours and unfunny jokes. Doesn't anyone in the organization let you come in with a clean slate?"

"Whoa, relax, Mel. I'm on your side. We're in the same boat you and me. It's just that I've been paddling longer. Ex-cop, ex-marine. Same difference. Everyone at Immigration's an ex-something. Just do your job well and let the guys see what you're made of. You'll get through it. You've got to expect the odd cop joke for the first few weeks. It's human nature."

Mel chewed the inside of his mouth. It tasted pretty good.

"You're right, Charlie. Sorry. I guess I get a bit touchy when I'm starving to death."

"How come you haven't eaten?"

"The orientation program. It's like boot camp. They run you through ten different jobs in a week and the schedule doesn't include eating or sleeping. They had me on a sweep last night, flophouses, parks, deserted buildings. It was a full night."

"Net anything?"

"Couple of Ukrainian hookers, Nigerians, the usual batch of Latinos. I don't know. By midnight it was all starting to blur. I couldn't tell a Vietnamese from a Pole. I'd been on shift since six that morning. When it was all over I was in sniffing range of a burger but I had to give it up for world peace."

Charlie was about to follow up on that when a little woman with either a bad perm or a cheap wig waddled over to their table. He thought she was selling something. She had two full shopping bags. He was about to shoo her away but she smiled at Mel.

"Hello, sir," she said.

Mel nodded, "Hi, Mrs. Asturias."

She laughed. "You remember my name. That is a good skill."

"And I wish I possessed it. It's the name of the hotel my wife and I spent our honeymoon."

She laughed again. "Then I hope it was good memory for you."

"Best part of the marriage."

"I pleased to hear it. Okay, gotta go."

"You eat here, Mrs. Asturias?"

She laughed again as if the possibility was somewhere out there between Saturn and the planet formerly known as Pluto. "Oh no, sir. Not me. I buy the lunch for my gentleman. His favourite. Bye now." She smiled at Charlie, "Bye, sir."

They watched her walk up to the counter and joke with the Filipino sushi chef.

"Friend of yours?" Charlie asked.

"Last formal interview for a green card. They've had me sitting in on them all week. Nice lady. Her and her husband. I chatted with them in the break."

"It doesn't pay to fraternize with the enemy."

"You could say the same to her, I guess."

"Think they'll get them? The cards?"

"They've got eight nephews back in Guatemala and between them there are some thirty billion grand nieces and nephews. Give those two green cards and you could repopulate Little Guatemala fifty times over. So, no, not a damned chance in Hell."

"That's not a policy you'd find written down anywhere, you realize?"

"Doesn't need to be. It's common sense."

"Cop's instinct?"

Mel glared at him. "Yeah! You want another sample?"

"Sure."

"You'll like this one. This 'get to know the new guy' lunch we're almost having here."

"What about it?"

"You know what my gut tells me?"

"It's empty?"

"Yeah, that too. But it tells me you've been delegated."

"Is that so?"

"It is. And it wouldn't surprise me if there wasn't a staff pool to cover your expenses."

"You really do have to let that superstitious cop mind of yours go."

"Really? Ex-cop, ex-marine, same difference. Instant bonding. Two guys who played with guns. Let's be pals. Know what? I don't think you're that fond of me. I think you kind of liked being the local tough guy and felt threatened when I rode into town. Get the dirt on him, you thought. Put him down. I bet you promised the team you'd get a few shots of Suntory into me over lunch and I'd feel this overwhelming urge to spew it all out. Kindred spirit relieving his burden."

Charlie frowned. Pushed his chopsticks around on the table to point at his adversary.

"And what burden would that be, Pilgrim?"

"Why I was kicked off the force."

"It didn't occur to me."

"Is that right?"

Charlie smiled as if he suddenly liked the guy sitting opposite him.

"I've got twenty bucks on you sleeping with someone's wife."

"You son of a . . ." Mel shook his head and laughed in the direction of the static waitresses.

"So, why were you?" Charlie ventured.

"Why?"

"Yeah."

"I shot a guy."

"I thought that's what cops did."

"Not at random. This was the wrong target. I missed the bad guy and shot the poor fool standing beside him. It was a mistake. I panicked."

"Kill him?"

"He lost a leg. Sued the city. See? Bad cop. Enough for you?" He stood, wiped his forehead with the tiny white towel and dropped it on the table. "Feel free to pass that news on with my compliments." He turned half away then looked back, "Who won?"

"Janice in filing."

"Lot of good talent wasted in filing."

"Going someplace?"

"Get something to eat."

Mel walked to the door and held it open for Mrs. Asturias. She thanked him and he followed her out into the street.

2.

She poked her tongue out through the corner of her lips as she turned the key slowly in the lock. That and squinting always seemed to stop the lock from creaking and the catch from clicking. He'd said it didn't matter if she made a noise. He said she could come in through the front wall with a pneumatic drill and it wouldn't disturb him. It might have been true but she wasn't about to try. He always seemed so peaceful there wrapped up in his silence. She remembered how the nuns used to stare at the cracks in the convent walls. They'd cradle their crucifixes in their hands and seem to suck in the silence all round them. Their smiles always made the young Violetta believe they'd done something rude and sinful during the night and were bathing joyfully in the memory of it.

He had that same smile, Mr. Yidam. She'd vacuumed around him once while he was meditating and he hadn't stirred. Not even the upholstery attachment made him blink and that had a whiney, annoying sound to it. Mr. Yidam was one of her more peculiar gentlemen. A twenty-five hundred a month luxury apartment. High-tech gadgets in the kitchen. State-of-the-art sound system with speakers in each of the nine rooms. A bath you could hold a regatta in and a refrigerator full of the most expensive deli items. But he didn't seem proud of any of it. He didn't even seem comfortable there. The Kennedy sofa and queen-sized mattress were still covered in the plastic they'd been delivered in. Mr. Yidam spent

211

most of his time sitting on the floor. She was sure he slept there too. A man-sized rectangle of fitted carpet had been pulled up to reveal the wooden boards.

To Violetta's eyes it was as if the man were living in a department store show-house and didn't want to get fingerprints on anything. The apartment was always spotless. She was genuinely embarrassed to collect the cleaning money each month. Naturally, she never refused it. They needed the money. They'd be getting their green cards soon, her and Miguel, and they had first option on a little place over in Cicero. Nothing fancy, a solid redbrick unit on a quiet street. Mr. Yidam was a generous man and never asked her to do any of the extramural tasks—baby sitting, shopping, repairing the waste-disposal unit—that the others assumed were in an illegal alien's job description. She was a registered illegal and would soon be legitimate, Miguel assured her of that, but until then she performed all her duties without complaint. Coming to Mr. Yidam's was one of her few pleasures.

She and Mr. Yidam had exchanged names, first and family, at their initial meeting. He was Mongolian but was resigned to being called a Chinaman. She was from Guatemala but had gotten used to being a Mexican. Whatever. If it helps get you through life . . . He confessed he'd never met a Guatemalan and insisted she tell him everything about her country. She was embarrassed how little she knew. She told him she'd never met a Mongolian and she had just as many questions, but it wasn't her place to ask. He was her employer. When she was with her husband late at night she'd talk about her mild-mannered Mongolian gentleman.

"One day I'll ask him," she said. "One day after we get our cards."

"Ask him what?"

"Why he's here. What he does."

"It's not our business."

"I'm curious."

"We need the money more than we need to satisfy our curiosity, Querida. Don't poke a stick at a sleeping dog," he'd said.

Miguel was right, yet Violetta felt no danger from her sleeping Mongolian dog. And although she would never be able to tell her husband, she had an entirely different sensation when she was near Mr. Yidam. She felt love. Not a romantic attachment. Mr. Yidam was as old as the ruins at Tikal. No, not that type of love. This was a physical sensation as if her heart were suddenly energized, capable of remarkable feats. She knew this was a feeling that emanated from her Mongolian gentleman and she knew that asking her questions would only serve to strengthen that feeling. Nothing bad could come of it. Today, she would ask. Today.

She put her coat and hat on the pegs inside the front door and carried her Tupperware container along the spacious hall. She walked past the living room where she expected to see him sitting cross-legged on the floor. He wasn't there. Neither was he in the kitchen. She looked into the study and the bedrooms and there was a marked absence of Mr. Yidam. This surprised her as she'd never been to the apartment when he wasn't in it. She shrugged and decided fate didn't want her to ask her questions today. She was a great believer in the influence of the fates on her life.

She realized she was still carrying her container and decided to put it in the kitchen before starting her unnecessary work. But as she passed the living room this second time she glanced in and her breath seemed to freeze in her chest. Mr. Yidam was there, sitting cross-legged in his usual position, a little Buddha deep in his happy meditation. She wondered how she could not have seen him there. He was as plain as her nose. And, as she stood in the archway staring at him his eyes sprang open already focused on her face. A jolt to her heart caused her to stumble backwards, not an unpleasant feeling but powerful. It had certainly not been her imagination.

"Mrs. Asturias," he said, "You're early."

There were no clocks in the apartment but he was correct. She had arrived ten minutes before her agreed time.

"I . . . I didn't see you there," she said, trying to calm her pulse. He rose elegantly like the unmelting of an ice sculpture and stepped toward her. He always appeared to be sincerely delighted to see her. In fact, everything she said or did seemed to fascinate him. It made her uncomfortable at times but it was a curiously addictive discomfort.

"You've brought me something," he beamed.

She looked first into his eyes, then at the plastic box in her hands.

"*Torrejas*," she said. "They are sweetbread and custard cakes from my country. I made them."

She handed them to Mr. Yidam. He peeled back the lid and looked up in delight.

"Then I think we shall drink percolated coffee and sit together and eat them . . . and rap," he said.

"Sir, I don't think . . ." she blushed.

"Please, I insist. You have so many questions."

She opened her mouth to decline but no sound came out. So, they sat at the kitchen table and she watched her small Mongolian employer eat with great relish. He wore the smallest size of Chicago Bears shirt, labeled FOR EIGHT TO TEN-YEAR-OLDS but it still hung off him like a dark blue dust cover. She'd been astounded by his wardrobe, all hip-hop and pro-sports. He didn't appear to own anything . . . appropriate. But he seemed content enough to look ridiculous.

They ate their first two torrejas in silence. She had to admit they were pretty damned good. Mr. Yidam wiped his mouth with a napkin.

"Your cooking has won me over," he said. "Feel free to ask me anything. I do not have the ability to lie although I have to work on that too."

She knew instinctively he was waiting for those important questions she had in her mind. Her heart told her. Her curiosity was simmering like hot fat, bubbling, fit to boil over.

"Why you are here?" she asked, astounded at her directness.

"I was sent. Banished, you might say." Her eyes registered that she didn't know the word. "Kicked out," he added.

"Mongolia kick you out?"

"Only my monastery . . . my church."

"You church kick you out, sir? You are a priest?"

"I was a monk. Yes."

"You did something bad?"

"Unforgivable. Yes, very bad."

"What?" Again she was shocked at her own brazenness. "I am sorry."

"No need to be, Mrs. Asturias. I am happy to tell you. Basically, it is this. I climbed the spiritual mountain that all monks . . . all religious people are climbing. I had a gift and I was able to climb higher and faster than the others, higher than the great priests, higher than the greatest lama. And I reached the top. I saw the view. I understood. And it was incredibly boring. Dull as mud. But I was there, home plate, World Series, and I had nowhere else to go. I had to rethink my life's philosophy. New plan. On the journey I had acquired skills. A righteous monk would have used those skills to do good."

"And you, no?"

"I developed a taste for gambling."

"Gambling? Like at the casinos?"

"More like horses . . . football games, things like that."

"And you lost?"

"Oh, no. If I had lost I would have been forgiven. I would have been accepted back into the monastery as a wounded yak. I would have been a cause. No, I had acquired skills that took the gamble out of gambling. I had learned that the future is happening now."

Mrs. Asturias collected their cups and went over to the machine for refills.

"I am sorry, sir. My English . . ."

"It isn't a problem of English, Mrs. Asturias. Even if I spoke fluent Spanish it would be difficult to understand. You see? You, and almost everyone on Earth see life as a straight line. It has a beginning and an end. Like the walking escalator at the airport, you step on, and when the journey is over you step off."

"Is not like that?"

"Not at all. Look!" He held up one of Mrs. Asturias' fine cakes. "Imagine life as a torreja. And you are a worm. No offence intended. You can enter and leave at any point. There is no beginning and no end to the torreja, only to your involvement with it. You swim around inside and at one point you get too close to the caramel and sweet-wine surface and you drop out. All over. Finished."

Mrs. Asturias was looking closely at her own torreja.

"So, how do you know what day it is?" she asked.

"What if they don't exist? Days? Months? Years? What if there is no such thing? We have been made to believe in them by man. Man who must have order and logic in his life to survive."

"I going a little crazy here. You say the future—no is the future?"

"What if all of it—what you call the future and the past—what if they are happening now, side by side? What if they are happening just as this, our conversation here, is happening? And what if you could develop the skill to leave and re-enter the torreja at any point? At some junctures events have taken place, at others they have not. Somewhere in that torreja you are still at school. Somewhere else you are living happily in old age back in Guatemala. All of those lives running alongside each other, present and past, bumping into each other all over the place. What we call coincidences are just collisions and crossovers, people making appearances like guests in TV episodes. Everybody affects everybody else. You don't realize how much interdependence there is if you don't have the skill."

"You have this skill?"

"Yes."

"You are here now?" She doubted her sanity that she should ask such a question.

"My body is here but we are only passengers in our bodies. With the right training our minds can step out and walk around. We can go to other levels where our bodies are also to be found. You are beginning to wish you hadn't asked."

She wasn't surprised he knew that.

"Sir, is a little difficult."

"I know. I'm sorry."

"But I see how you can cheat at gambling."

"Excellent."

"You just step into the tomorrow, but it ain't really tomorrow, and you look at the newspaper."

"Quite right, Mrs. Asturias. It should have taken the fun out of it but I got a lot of pleasure out of making money dishonestly. It set me off on a whole new path. I had reached the great light at the end of my religion and was plunged into a vast depression. So I had a tremendous thirst to study some other doctrine. I chose sin. I even put in a request for a grant from my abbot. That's when the gambling story came to light and I was thrown out. I decided to embark along this new path independently, funded from my winnings. I believe it is vital to study all of the doctrines to be able to be truly objective."

"You no see me in America?"

"I'm sorry?"

"You say somewhere I am a old lady in Guatemala. You see me there and no here?"

"Yes."

She frowned. "I don't get no green card?"

"No."

"Miguel's gonna be pissed about that."

"But not you."

"I miss my country. Better be poor and happy than rich and sad."

"Quite right."

"You want some more coffee, sir?"

"No, thanks. I've just had a sudden urge for a strawberry Slurpee," he said. "You see, I'm entering into this study very gently. Today a Slurpee at the 7-Eleven, tomorrow vice and drugs."

Mr. Yidam climbed from his chair and went over to the coat hooks. He put on his Bears top coat. It hung to his shins.

"Can I get you anything?" he asked.

Violetta was chewing on the last of her world.

"I ate too much already."

"Go on, special day. My treat."

"Okay," she smiled. "You know what a corn dog is?"

1.

The little Asian guy ambled over to the cashier with a strawberry Slurpee in his right hand and a corn dog in his left.

Life as a Torreja

A look at time, connectivity and coincidence, this one; seven short stories within a short story all joined together with seen and unseen threads.

Of all the stories, this one was the most pleasure to write, and the most difficult. I was sittin' in front of a 7/11 in Carolina one night, killing time till 1 a.m. In a half-hour spell I spotted at least twenty fascinating characters. None of them knew the others. None of them spoke. But I knew they all had interesting tales to tell. As I sat on the train later that night, I started to wonder how deep you would have to dig to find connections between them all. And what if the connections weren't deep at all? What if they, and I, were all meant to be there in front of the 7/11? And that got me thinking about time (there isn't much to do on the night train to D.C.)

I wanted to play around with the concept of time in a story - or, rather, do away with it completely. What if our pasts aren't chronologically behind us? If our futures aren't ahead? What if they're running along in tandem with 'now' - side by side like lawn-mower rotors? Imagine a hall of mirrors, thousands of images of ourselves spread out like wings; to the right we get progressively older, to the left, younger. But it's all happening now. No? I tell you what. Have a couple of glasses of wine. It helps.

Collecting Old Footprints

I REMEMBER THE day Yai left home. It was a Saturday in May 1985, and the rains blowing in from Burma on the tail of a cyclone had finally left us behind. *Yai* is Thai for grandmother, but all the time I was growing up I'd seen it more as a name. It suited her somehow. I hadn't really expected to see her there at eight in the morning. She rarely got out of bed before midday. But she was walking bright and light across the hallway on her way to the open front door. The morning sun was throwing beams in through the doorway this way and that, but I could make out she was wearing her best frock, the one with the Liberty print she'd brought back from England on her last trip. She was carrying a heavy-looking suitcase.

I called out, "Yai, you want any help with that?" But she ignored me. Either that or she didn't have her hearing aid plugged in. She was naughty, either leaving it off and having an excuse not to listen to my mother's lectures, or pretending it was off and secretly listening to people talk about her. You could never tell with Yai. I tried again, "Yai, I could run down and get you a motorcycle taxi at the corner. It's hot already. You don't want to lug that bag all the way . . ."

She stopped and looked back at me. I don't know whether it was a trick of the light or the result of a dip into the paints and pastels of her makeup box, but she looked rather sweet that morning. A happy face. Even when she smiled, her teeth seemed to fit in her mouth without sliding sideways. She'd always said that false teeth of a size to fit her made her look like a horse. So, against my mother's express orders, she'd spent her money on a set half the size. The teeth it contained were daintier, Yai argued, more like her own teeth before the sweet demons took them. But my mother told her they made her look like she had a half-eaten extra-strong mint between her gums. Yai had always been a disappointment to my mother.

But Yai's teeth seemed to fit, the morning she left. She lifted a finger to her lips to shush me, gave me a little wave, and I watched her walk through the door to be eaten up by the rays of the sun. I imagine other families with live-in grannies might have been surprised to see them leave home, but our Yai wasn't the type you could tie down. I suppose with rope it might have been possible, but even with her little false incisors she would have chewed through her bindings and escaped in time to be playing cards by mid-afternoon. That was her main vice. She had several subsidiary vices—vices she wouldn't even acknowledge as sinful—but her main addiction was poker.

Although her original pool of friends was whittling itself down, she had ingratiated herself into a new generation of players and drinkers. The no-need-to-actually-work offspring of the wealthy old Chinese families, the wives of criminals and politicians (often interchangeable), the new entrepreneurs making a mint from sales to tourists at the Night Bazaar. These were her cronies. No circle of gentle ladies playing for sea shells or matchsticks, these. This was a coterie of brandy-drinking, big-money-spending fanatics. And our Yai was the godmother of the gang. She didn't always come home. She might be away for two or three days when the group was in high song and the baht were flowing. We never knew where the stakes came from to keep her active in such circles. My father assumed she had a secret cache of my grandfather's savings in a chest buried in the back garden, but we didn't ever see a brass *satang* of it. If she had money it was hers.

Yes, money was another of my mother's issues with Yai. We weren't the poorest family in Chiang Mai, not by a long stretch. Dad worked with the Forestry Department. Mum taught primary school at Wat Buak Krok Noi. So there was always money coming in. Just not from the direction of the back bedroom. Mum's favourite line to Yai was, "You treat our house like a hotel but you never clean the slate at the end of the month." Dad tried to remind mum about her filial duties to the woman who had made sacrifices for her only daughter for all those years. Mum reminded him back that once her husband passed away, Yai had spent much of her life on holiday with a succession of temporary suitors. My mother, in turn, had been dumped with a criminal lineup of maids of dubious quality. She didn't bear witness to a great deal of sacrifice. You see? By rights I should have been a troubled child. Such an undercurrent of animosity and hostility all around me. I'm not sure how I made it through those years. I give a lot of credit to my year-two teacher, Miss Somphon. In my report card she wrote, "Punnika has a unique gift for assessing a problem and determining what is correct and what is incorrect." She'd been talking about physics but I adopted it as a description of me, philosophically, from the point of view of a fourteen-year-old Thai girl dealing with life. I embroidered the message and hung it over my bed.

Apart from a lack of positive role-models and an absent grandmother, another problem I needed to assess at the time was the arrival of Koko. This was one of Yai's little surprises, one she'd sprung a few days before her departure. She'd come down to lunch wearing her familiar dark glasses, her hair in a bold red turban. She staggered a little on her way to the table.

"Goodness sake, Mother," mum had said. "You look like an Indian fortune teller. I hope you aren't planning to go out in public looking like that."

Yai smiled to reveal her dentures nestling on the left side of her mouth.

"Care to know where you're headed, dear?" she said, lifting the plastic food covers one at a time and sniffing at mum's cooking.

"Ha! You, seeing the future? That's funny," mum said. "With those things on you can't even see the table in front of you."

"I can see well enough to know the pork isn't properly cooked."

"Why? Because it isn't burnt black the way you prepare it?"

See what I had to put up with? It was like being an umpire at a cock fight, except the cocks were hens, all barbs and flying feathers. I was sure at the time that if ever I took the trouble to get married and was unfortunate enough to produce a daughter, I would take her back to the hospital and exchange her for a boy.

Yai decided that was the perfect moment to surprise us with her dog revelation.

"This house would benefit greatly from having a dog," she'd said.

I could see my mother wrestle for a connection to overcooked pork, but when it became clear Yai was suggesting we adopt a puppy, my mother went through, first the roof, then a litany of reasons why our house would not be appropriate. But her arguments were moot. Yai had already made a selection from the litter of one of her cronies and we could expect the delivery that afternoon. She won her victory with an underhanded move, telling us that any puppies not found a home that day would be taken to the Ping River and drowned. Mum clenched her teeth and her fists which made it very difficult for her to eat lunch.

As mum had to take me to volleyball practice that afternoon, neither of us was around to join the reception committee. When we returned in the evening, Koko was sitting on the front step, confused as only a two-month-old Terrier/Alsatian mix can be, excited and terrified all at once. Mum stepped over her and left the official welcome to me. At first sight, she was a nervous cute little button, but we were soon to learn that Koko had what the psychiatrists refer to as schizophrenia. I confess I had to look it up when dad first made the comment but he really hit the nail on the head. Sometimes she'd be friendly and playful like the toilet tissue dogs on television. Other times she was a villain. And I don't mean naughty. I'm talking about sly, potentially homicidal. At times she'd be whining pitifully, begging for food. I'd put out a bowl of canned sardines and rice and she'd turn up her nose at it. Make me feel I'd insulted her dignity. Go off and eat disgusting things she'd dug up from the flower beds.

I assumed she'd had a troubled childhood, but in spite of my own confused youth we weren't able to bond, or, at least, our bonding moments were rare and unexpected. Like on the morning Yai walked out on us. It was a Saturday, I remember. No school but a volleyball game in the afternoon against the spoilt bitches at Dara Academy. Mum and dad had left early for a mixed-double pétanque tournament. I'd seen Yai leave and I was about to chase after her but it occurred to me my sleepwear was too sexy for the street. I ran back to my room and changed, but by the time I got to the front gate Yai was long gone. I was stupid. Of course she'd have one of her gang members come to collect her.

We had a front and back yard with lots of greenery. Dad was always bringing home chunks of jungle from work and our house was overgrown, soon to be eaten up completely by the forest. I turned to see Koko cowering under a bougainvillea bush. That morning I'd put out a bowl of last night's leftovers on the back step. Okay, not five-star dining I admit, but a good helping of nutritious scraps. Yet now she was giving me this hangdog look as if she hadn't eaten for months. She was in her passive-submissive persona that morning. She waddled up to me with her ears flat and her tail wagging down by her back paws. I knelt and she walked straight into me as if she had her eyes closed.

"You saw Yai leave, did you Ko? Is that why you're looking so sad?"

She whined. I didn't speak dog but I took this to mean yes.

"Looks like she's dumped you with us, little lady. Not that she had much to do with you when she was here."

I had a flash in my mind of Yai leaving my mum with the disreputable maids and I decided right then and there I'd do all I could to be the perfect mother to our little orphan, no matter how screwed up she was.

No toddlers were perfect. As a special treat I went to the kitchen and found her some old wafer biscuits. She ate them the way a vacuum cleaner sucks up polystyrene bubbles then looked at me for more. She was going to be a difficult child.

There was a radio station, FM100, out of Chiang Mai University. Dad listened to it all the time. Unless there was a Royal Broadcast or an international boxing event involving a Thai, our television sat without expression and unplugged in the corner of the living room. The outside world came to us through the wireless. There was music, the occasional political discussion, household hints, and community service announcements. One of the latter arrived each evening from the information department at Maharat Hospital. Every now and then they'd try to find the relatives of concussion victims or some sad old man they'd found walking the streets with dementia. From time to time they'd have the gory duty of announcing that an unidentified body had been found. They'd give the estimated age and a description of whatever there was left to describe.

All three of us, me, Mum and Dad, were in the kitchen. Dad had invaded the kitchen table and was working on a landscaping plan that hung like a tablecloth off two sides. Mum was at the stove making a banana custard sweet. I was crushing garlic in a mortise. None of us was actually listening to the radio. It was just part of the soundscape; the neighbour's chickens, Koko growling and digging up the roots of dad's frangipani in the backyard, the bubbling of the coconut milk, the clunking of the pestle. But all of those sounds seemed to stop at the same time when the announcement was made.

". . . to be in her late sixties, slight build, wearing a pale-blue pant suit."

The description continued with the make and registration of the motorcycle she'd been riding and the location of the accident. Dad looked at mum. The spoon dropped from her hand into the pot and splashed sweet coconut milk up the wall. The ants would have a party that night.

Dad's old Austin pulled up beside the house. I'd heard the sound thousands of times before but never had it turned my stomach so. I couldn't force myself to leave the table. My hands seemed to be super-glued to the wood. I waited for mum and dad to come back into the kitchen but only dad made it that far. I heard their bedroom door slam and mum burst into tears behind it. They'd come from the morgue. Dad sat beside me, put one of his big boney hands on my trembling one and nodded. Tears gushed out of my eyes as if a water pot had broken in my head. I couldn't speak. I could tell dad was choked up too. So we sat like that for something like ten minutes until dad squeezed my hand and went to mix us a strawberry cordial. It was something he used to do when I was little and fell off my bike or grazed my elbow. It tasted even better the day we discovered Yai was dead.

"There's just one thing we're confused about, baby," he said. "Are you sure it was Saturday you saw her leave, and not Friday?"

"I'm certain. It was the day you and mum were playing pétanque. Yai and I were here alone. Why?"

"Well, it's just . . . it's just that the accident . . ." I'd never known dad to be stuck for words before. He started again. "She had a big poker game by all accounts. It finished at 2 a.m. She borrowed the hostess's spare motorcycle without asking. The woman didn't notice it was gone. Nobody knows where Yai was heading. She was drunk. She crashed into a post box in front of the university. But, baby, that was Friday night. She was already in the morgue long before eight on Saturday morning."

I let the abbot go through his rigmarole, the chanting and the incense burning, the supplication in front of a shiny gold Buddha perched up on a platform, and I knelt politely on the plastic mat with my hands together. The old monk had the face and build of a man who would have broken a lot of hearts in his life if he hadn't dedicated sixty years to the study of Buddhism. I'd been raised a Buddhist but I was a teenager going through all the doubts and disbeliefs teenagers are expected to go through. Religion was high on my list of suspicious activities. Until that time, I'd also had a healthy skepticism about the spirit world. But Yai had died early Saturday morning, as the death certificate and four witnesses confirmed. Six hours later

I saw her in the living room wearing her Liberty print dress and carrying a suitcase. There was little doubt I had encountered my first ghost. I didn't like it, not at all. Once you open that gate all kinds of unacceptables come running through. But I was determined to understand it.

Like most monks in the north, the abbot at Wat U Mong was multi-skilled in a number of branches of the occult. There was a lot of cross-over with fortune telling and exorcisms and blessing aircraft and army tanks. I'd first met this hip old man on a school visit. He'd told my class that the only reason there were more Buddhist monks than shamans was because you were less likely to be hit by a car if you wore saffron. I liked that. I'd vowed that day, if I had any spiritual turmoil, this was the man I'd come to see. And after my close encounter with my deceased grandmother I was a whirlwind of turmoil.

He rounded off his little ceremony with a high, palm-together wai and finally gave me his undivided attention. I told him about Yai. He showed no surprise whatsoever.

"It's common enough," he said.

"Seeing dead people walk out of your house is common?" I asked.

"In this case, yes. Nobody told your grandmother she was dead. If she'd been picked up by the body collection services or taken to a temple straight away, there would have been a small ceremony, a sort of orientation for the dispossessed soul. But nobody claimed the body. It was taken directly to the morgue. Your grandmother's spirit was confused. It's been running through its old routines for the last three days."

"You honestly believe that? The ghost of old Yai throwing down a full-house at a gambling den and knocking back Regency Brandy, totally oblivious of the fact she didn't have a body any more?"

There were much more polite ways to address a respected monk, but you have to remember I was still in shock at that stage. He fielded my rudeness well. He smiled and said, "Well, I doubt it's quite as Disney as that but there is ample evidence to suggest it isn't all total buffalo dung. And you have to admit, you did see her."

I had to admit that. I didn't want to, but I had no choice.

"Will I see her again?" I asked.

"Do you have any unfinished business?"

"I just . . . I didn't get to say goodbye. That's all."

"Then, as nobody else saw her, we would have to assume she was fond of you. Now her body has been claimed and the cremation ceremonies have begun, her spirit should be settled. There are those who say that on the seventh day of the death of its host, the spirit is preparing for the journey. It returns to a place or a person it loved in life and collects its old footprints as a souvenir. That is often a moment when you can spend some time together."

Of course it was ridiculous. Collecting its old foot-prints? Whatever next? But on the following Saturday I made an excuse to miss the volleyball tournament in Lampang and spent the day in the small pavilion, the *sala* in our backyard. Yai had loved it there. She spent more time in the garden sala than in her own room. She would hang in her hammock strung between the bamboo posts reading her magazines, sipping her lemon tea, listening to the wind charms that captured every breeze and regurgitated it in song.

I swung back and forth waiting for her with a book open on my lap. Koko was in one of her satanic moods, gnawing on the bamboo slats, biting my bottom through the thinning hammock cloth, barking at birds. Some days I loved her dearly. Others I felt like digging a deep hole and burying her in the dirt. That day I spent waiting for Yai was one of the 'Where's the shovel?' days. She gave me no peace.

"I just do not understand that animal," mum had said, putting down a lunch tray on the sala table. I'd convinced her I was studying for an English exam and couldn't possibly leave the pavilion all day.

"She must have been a racehorse in a previous life, that dog. She's all over the place," mum continued. "One minute she's hounding me at the back door. Then, I walk through the house and there she is exhausted at the front."

I stayed in the sala all afternoon and evening. Dad connected the electric lamp and put down mosquito coils for me. Both my parents had been dumfounded but delighted to see that my foreign language block had cleared itself and they wanted to encourage the born-again linguist in me. Normally they'd insist on me being in bed before ten but my enthusiasm carried over to them. I noticed them take one last peek at me through their bedroom window before turning out the light and going to bed. Apart from one lightning toilet break, I sat in the sala for nineteen hours that day, but I didn't see Yai. I was terribly sad. I was sure she'd come to collect her footprints from the sala and stay for a chat. I blamed Koko. They say dogs can see spirits and I assumed her bad manners that day had kept Yai away from me. But it turns out there was another reason.

The next morning I was bent into the shape of a banana from the hammock. Bits of me clicked when I tried to stand up straight. I walked into the kitchen to find mum deliberating over a bowl of rice porridge. She seemed to be debating whether or not to eat what was on her spoon. She didn't notice me until I was sitting opposite her.

"Hello, baby," she said at last and then asked in English, "How are you?"

It took me a while to realize what she'd said, then a moment more to find an appropriate answer.

"I'm fine."

"What time did you finally get to bed?" Thankfully she'd settled back into a friendly language.

"Midnight."

She seemed delighted. "Oohoo! We'll have you in the university in no time if you carry on like this."

I hoped she wouldn't insist on giving me a test. I needed a diversion.

"You don't look like you slept much yourself," I said.

"Odd dream," she said.

I went to the cupboard and said good morning to my instant cup noodles. I remember I had reached a generational crossroads at the time. I loved rice porridge but it was imperative to be seen as cool and international. So I ate and wore things that didn't agree with me just to fit in with my generation. I imagine fourteen-year-olds are still doing that today. I didn't hurry to boil the water or rejoin mum at the table because, quite frankly, I was afraid she'd tell me about her dream. I'd had enough weirdness for one year.

She told me anyway.

"I saw Yai last night," she said.

I was astounded.

"Where?"

"In my sleep. At least I assume it was. But it seemed so real."

I abandoned my soaking noodles and sat at the table with her. I felt I'd made a considerable investment in this case and I wanted to hear everything.

"I'm listening," I said.

"There's not much to tell, really. It was one of those could-be-asleep, could-be-awake moments. You know? You wake up and you see something and you react the way you would normally. Then something tells you this can't be real and you realize it's a dream?"

I had no idea what she was talking about.

"Yes," I said.

"So, it was the middle of the night. I woke up, or not, I'm not sure. You had the light on in the sala so the room was still partially lit from outside. Your father was snoring beside me. I assumed it was his grunting that woke me. I squeezed his nostrils together to shut him up. It always works. But, just as I was getting back to sleep, I saw something moving over by the door. I lifted my head and I asked, 'Who is it?' There was clearly somebody on the floor on their hands and knees. I couldn't make out what they were doing. I said, 'Who are you? What are you doing here?' And who should look up at me but my mother? '*Mae*?' I said, 'What are you doing down there on the floor?' She didn't answer me. She just continued to do whatever it was she was doing, working closer and closer to the bed. Don't forget I was in this nowhere world between asleep and awake. I was getting impatient with her. I wanted her to finish whatever it was and go back to bed. 'That's the last of them,' she said.

"She got to her feet and leaned over me. She was cradling something in her arms.

'What do you have there, mae?' I asked her. But she didn't answer.

'You really should lock your bedroom door,' she said. 'Do you know how many times I've crept in here in the early hours of the morning and watched you sleep?'

'Why would you watch me sleep?' I asked.

'A mother's pride,' she said.

'You do talk in riddles,' I told her, but I suppose, at that moment, you turned out the light in the sala and the room was dark. Yai had vanished into the shadows. When I woke this morning I was still certain it had actually happened. But of course . . ."

I saw the tears well up in my mother's eyes. My noodles were cooling to a soggy mess on the sideboard but I knew it was time to tell her about my visit to Wat U Mong and the story of the spirits coming to collect their footprints from a place or a person they love. Whether Yai actually stopped in to look at her forty-year-old daughter as she slept is almost irrelevant. The important thing is that, spiritually, she did. And the fact she chose my mum's room to collect her footprints says a lot about her feelings. Mum was kind of mixed after that. She was happy, but she missed her mother even more. Of course I forgave Yai for not visiting me in the sala. She had her priorities right. I even apologized to Koko. And thereby hangs yet another tale.

Once all of her friends and gambling cohorts learned of my grandmother's demise, there was a grand procession of visitors to our house. We were astounded at the type of company she kept. Characters from the magazine society pages sat in our little living room telling us outrageous stories of my Yai, professing their loss at her passing. There were so many wreaths sent to us the house stunk of flowers for a month. But of all the visitors and messages, there was one that made all the other events of that month seem positively normal.

We got a telephone call from a lady who lived in Mae Rim. She had just returned from the Bahamas and heard about our Yai's death. She was terribly sorry and wondered whether we would like to return the dogs.

I heard my dad attempt to correct and then clarify the content of the phone conversation. No, it was not a mistake. Yai had ordered, not one, but two dogs from the lady. They were not orphans doomed for a dip in the Ping River, but pedigree pups with all the mental handicaps inbred animals display. I had been wrong about the cross-breeding. Dad put down the phone and told us we should go out into the yard and find Koko. I found her first in her regular spot by the sala chewing up a shirt that had previously hung from the washing line. Mum found the second Koko deep in the bushes. She had made a nest and appeared to be living largely on bugs.

We called the lady back and she explained. As the parents were almost identical (for breeding purposes) the litter was also clone-like. Yai had chosen the chief bitch and the runt at the bottom of the pecking order. They had as much in common as me and the English language. The bitch was territorial and aggressive. The runt was scared to death of her, not daring to venture into her domain in the backyard, not being allowed anywhere near the feeding bowl. I could imagine Yai selecting the pair and having a chuckle at how much it would inconvenience my mother.

We held up the two dogs, identical in every way apart from their souls. We returned the bitch to her owner who sold her for an impressive sum of money, and hung on to the runt. Mum had christened her Somsri. That was Yai's real name and a totally inappropriate name for a dog, but she didn't seem to object. She grew to be a strong and loving animal and continued to live with mum and dad even after I moved out. I would often stop by the house and catch my mother chatting with the dog in the back yard. Somsri, her ear cocked, listening to mum and never once answering back or showing disrespect. Mum loved her very much and the grateful animal remained a trusted member of the family for twenty-two years.

Somsri died last night in her sleep, which is probably why I'm writing down this memoir today. Mum phoned early this morning. She was remarkably calm considering how close she and the dog had been. She invited me to stay over at the house next Friday. That would be the seventh day after Somsri's death. She thought I might like to spend the night with her drinking hot chocolate in the sala. Somsri had always loved that place so much. And, who knows? She might need to gather a few paw prints to take with her to heaven.

Collecting Old Footprints

My wife, Jessi, is from Chiang Mai. Her relatives used to be in the coffin business (no dying profession jokes from me here). That combination naturally leads a lot of ghost stories. Some, Jessi believes. Others, she just tells me to scare the bewillywops out of me. I'm a big fan of the supernatural although, to my great regret, I don't have any personal experiences.

I lived in a haunted house in the south of Laos for two years and I was the only one in the village who didn't see the old general with no arms, who lived here with me (no 'armless' jokes...)

This story was based on one of Jessi's recollections of her grandmother who saw one of her sons walk out of the house one morning. She called out but he didn't respond. In fact the son had died in an accident a few days before. People in the north believe that if you dream of somebody walking out of the house and ignoring you, they're either deaf or dead as a door nail.

Although I've made it more literal, the expression 'gep roy taaw' (collect footprints) applies to ghosts seen in places they used to frequent, picking up their old memories to take with them to Nirvana.

A slightly embellished true story from the Gulf of Siam.

WE MOVED
TO THE
SOUTH,
TO THE
GULF,
TO THE
COAST
WHERE THE
BLOATED
MARCH SUN
MADE US
ROAST,
MADE US
TOAST.
A DIP IN
THE SEA?
WELL,
WHY NOT
HAVE A GO?
BUT HOW
COULD
I KNOW
WHAT WAS
LURKING
BELOW
?

OUR NEIGHBOUR, SUKHON
WAS 103
SHE WAS BORN
ON THE SAND
LIVED HER LIFE
BY THE SEA
I WENT TO
HER HUT
SAID 'HELLO'
MADE A WAI. →
SHE GAVE ME
A HUG
(VERY ODD
FOR A THAI)
I TOLD HER
STRAIGHT OUT
I WAS PLANNING
A SWIM
AND, SOONER THAN
THROW MYSELF IN
ON A WHIM

I WANTED TO
KNOW
IF SOME CREATURE
MIGHT
SNAP ME,
DEVOUR
OR DISMEMBER
OR POISON
OR ZAP ME

She told me,
"My dear
in ten decades
plus three
not once have
I met
any dangers
at sea.
I have all
my limbs
and my skin
is unscarred.
I've never
been threatened.
I'm never
on guard."

So,
armed with
this knowledge
I went
back next door
and ran
to the ocean
with 4 on the
floor.
And dived in
the water
and frolicked
and splashed
'til in front
of my eyes

A GREAT
JELLY FISH
FLASHED

SHE WRAPPED
HERSELF ROUND
ME
A TINGLING MESH

INJECTED HER
POISON DARTS
INTO MY FLESH

I CRIED A PROFANCTORY
FOUR-LETTER WORD,
CALLED OUT IN AGONY.
NOBODY HEARD.
FIRE IN MY VEINS
FROM THE WATER
I FLED
MY POOR EPIDERMIS
ALL BLOATED
AND RED,
SECONDS TO LIVE
NOT A MOMENT
TO PONDER
I BUNDLED MY WIFE AND ME
INTO THE HONDA.

AT THE DISTRICT
E.R.
I HAD
BARELY A CHANCE
SO, THE DOCTOR
INSISTED
I PAY IN
ADVANCE
BUT THE GODS
WERE BESIDE ME.
MY LIFE
IT WAS SPARED
WITH ONLY MY
SPEECH
AND MY WALLET
IMPAIRED

MY BODY
RECOVERED
MY LIMBS WERE
RETRAINED
MY HEART
FOUND ITS
BEAT

BUT THE TRAUMA
REMAINED

THERE WAS ONLY
ONE WAY
TO REMOVE ANY DOUBT
AS TO WHY
THE GREAT OCEAN
HAD SINGLED ME OUT

I SAT
IN THE HUT
OF MY NEIGHBOUR
SUKHON.
I DRANK
HER RICE WHISKY
UNTIL MY NOSE SHONE
AND FINALLY
ASKED HER
JUST HOW COULD IT BE
THAT THE SEA
HAD CLAIMED ME
BUT HAD NOT
TROUBLED SHE.

"WHY
SILLY YOUNG WHITE
MAN,"
SHE SAID
WITH A GRIN
"I'VE NEVER BEEN
BIT
CAUSE I'VE NEVER
BEEN IN.
WE LOCALS
AREN'T DESPERATE
TO LOSE
LIFE AND LIMB,
SO NOBODY
BOTHERED
TO TEACH ME
TO SWIM."

A Slightly Embellished True Story From the Gulf of Siam

In early 2008, my wife, Jess, and I left Chiang Mai, a polluted, sprawling ex-paradise in the north, and came to live in a place I shall not name (for fear of causing a rush) in the south: palm trees, boats, twenty kilometer round-trip bicycle ride to the post office, septic tanks, wells, flies, snakes, bats, bees, pigs, mosquitoes... and jellyfish. It was our idea of heaven.

If any of you remember the old TV show, Green Acres with Eddie Albert and Eva Gabor, you'll have an idea of what life is like for us (albeit without the "being extremely rich" sub-plot). We're still a bit naive as to local wiles but we're getting there. We're very fond of the people down here and two extended families have adopted us like stray dogs. We're addressing the karma issue by adopting street dogs.

The jellyfish incident was more embarrassing than life-threatening. I asked our neighbour, Auntie Sukhon whether I should be wary of the sea. She told me in all her years on the beach, she never been bitten. It was only after my return from hospital that she told me her secret. It's my fault. It transpires I'm allergic so I have to stay in my kayak in jelly season. No problem with crabs, so far.

I probably broke several golden rules of poetry in this piece. I know, for certain I violated the English language. I can't say I really care. I'm a fan of the old, "It's gotta rhyme or it ain't a real poem" school. I love the exercise of stretching the realms of possibility to force two otherwise antisocial words to pair up. Hang grammar. I'm not expecting a laureateship - nor do I honestly believe that's an actual word.
It's just a bit of fun.

Coconuts

'LOVE' WASN'T A word a man in Paak Nam would consider using to describe his relationship with his wife. The fact he didn't use it might have led you to believe he didn't feel it, and, as you'd never get him caught up in a dialogue on the topic, that might have been the truth too. That foolish Western penchant for confessing and broadcasting 'love', real or imagined, hadn't made it to the east coast of Thailand. In the department stores of Phuket they sold inflatable hearts on sticks for two months either side of Valentine's day. Wealthy MBA graduates hired airplanes to etch a vapor-trail FOR LOVE that vanished almost instantaneously in the polluted Bangkok sky. But men in Paak Nam were more likely to express a heartfelt admiration for the sleek form of a neighbour's cow than pass on a compliment to their wives.

Now, lovers? That was a different matter altogether. Flattery was a necessary evil when courting a minor wife in the wilds of Chumphon Province. Between fishing for squid, harvesting the abundant coconuts, or tending their oil palms, few men in Paak Nam were truly poor. You might go so far as to call them comfortably off. With a little diligence, hard work, and dedication, the men of Paak Nam might have all become wealthy. But, why be wealthy when you can be comfortable? Why labour twelve hours a day when you could lay back in your hammock and contemplate the lapping ocean? As a result of this laid-back, gently rocking attitude, Paak Nam men had neither money nor jewels to lavish on their prospective lovers. They had to resort to smiles and pretty words.

Gai had neither the money nor the smile nor the vocabulary to win a concubine. He was in his mid sixties, burnt to a dark crisp veneer by the Gulf sun, and wiry and gnarled as a bamboo root. He'd carried a gimp right leg since birth and was loath to use a dozen words when one well-placed grunt would do as well. Yet, despite all his failings, Gai had a mistress as well as a wife. If the truth were to be told, his life would have been happier without either. He enjoyed the winks and hoots from the local men who, in their own peculiar misogynistic ways, had begun to respect him. Buffoons who'd made fun of him all his life, now admired him. For this he could thank June, barely turned forty, ripe and rough as a fresh durian, generously accommodating on the mattress. But he often wondered whether she was worth it. Could he ever really enjoy her puddingy thighs while Jinda, his wife of thirty years, sat expressionless in the other room?

It had been five years since he'd made ... whatever Paak Nam men made to their wives. He'd tried. The doctor assured him he had a moral right. This was the same doctor who'd been accused of fiddling with high-school girls, but Gai had tried anyway. It had been impossible, almost embarrassing. He'd returned to bathing Jinda's lifeless naked body and attending to her ablutions in the mechanical, distant way you'd milk a cow. And all the while an angry resentment built within him. How dare she deny him his conjugal rights? How dare she turn him into a nursemaid? How could she have been so stupid? Her. Raised on a palm plantation. Felled by a coconut. Her skull split from ear to ear. She should have read the signs, instinctively known which nuts were ripe and ready to fall, even on a moonless night in July.

They'd attended a funeral, Gai and Jinda. The rice whisky hooch was warm from the still. On their way home, Gai had ridden them off the road and into a ditch. They'd giggled, lying on their sides in the tall grass beneath the motorcycle. They'd had neither the coordination to free themselves nor the sense to notice the pain. Such was the magic of local rice liquor. Gai had come around some hours later, alone with the Honda Dream still pinning his ant-bitten body to the ground. The throbbing hurt had reached his hip. The effects of the whisky had evaporated but its after-effects were crusted in his skull. He had no idea what had happened to his wife. He was angry with her for leaving him there. With no strength to retrieve the bike by himself, he'd limped home in a black mood and taken to his mattress.

They'd found Jinda an hour after sunrise, lying beneath a forty-foot coconut palm, the brown nut beside her like a spare head. They assumed she'd decided to walk home and that the god of mathematical odds had some grudge against her. You could stand directly beneath a coconut tree for a month and not be hit, or, on a bad day, two nuts might fall on you within a minute. It had only taken one to crack her skull. She'd lost a lot of blood and the young doctor at Paak Nam hospital hadn't held out much hope for her. As it turned out, the little hope he invested in the broken-headed woman proved to be a curse rather than a cure. She survived—the shell of her at least—and Gai had been allowed to take her home. He wasn't given the option of leaving her in the ward or propped up in a store cupboard. They gave him a crash-course in how to keep his wife sanitary, fill her up and empty her out. But they didn't tell him what to do with his life now he was married to a turnip.

Then, one hot day five years later, June arrived at his wife's plantation. He was spearing the thick-skinned nuts onto a spike and wrenching off the husks. They didn't surrender without a fight. He had a customer in Lang Suan who paid well for the small sand-brown shells and their protein-rich water. But, to get to them through the tough outer casing, a coconut harvester had to have great will and the hands of a gorilla. Gai threw another nut into the basket and noticed the lusciously curved woman watching him.

"You're very strong," June said.

Gai smiled with embarrassment.

"How's your wife?" She added.

"Who are you?"

"I'm Sakhon's cousin."

He spent a considerable time programming this information before, "The nurse?"

"Nursing assistant. Just got back from Bangkok. I heard you might need a hand."

But Gai ended up with far more than a hand. In the beginning, June came by twice a day to bathe Jinda while Gai tended the plantation. He paid her in coconuts and vegetables from the garden, pretty-coloured shellfish dredged from the beach, prawns with broken radar who headed into shallow water thinking it was the deep ocean. But her own family had the same options, the same barter system, and she didn't seem to need any of the offerings he attempted to make.

He couldn't work out exactly what it was she wanted. He'd been astounded when she first made her play for him in the back bedroom. He'd been tempted to ask her what was wrong with her. Didn't she have any taste? She had her fair share of men to choose from in Paak Nam and any one of them had more to offer than Gai. Or so he thought. No. In fact, perhaps he didn't think at all, not until it was too late. Perhaps he just let events roll over and toss him around like a rogue wave. Yes, a bit of thinking back then mightn't have been a bad thing.

When they were still happy, in bed with his wife, Gai had felt like the hungry neighbourhood poacher allowed to cross the fence and pilfer a mango when it took his fancy. June, on the other hand, delivered her mangoes in a pick-up truck and stayed up all night steaming sticky rice in coconut milk to bring out the flavour. She gave sex a brand new definition in Gai's mind. He became addicted at first to it, then to June. In the early days they had been respectful of the barely-living body of Jinda. They hadn't shown each other affection in front of her. They reserved their saucy conversations for the small bamboo pavilion in front of the house and had their physical relations in the back bedroom.

But after several months, Jinda's status in the house receded until it fell somewhere between that of the transistor radio and a rice pot. This transformation happened so gradually Gai didn't actually notice that his wife had ceased to be a person. There was no longer any embarrassment in her company. He and June talked openly about whatever took their fancy and even made love on the family bed once or twice with Jinda lying on her sleeping mat across the room. It was on one such occasion that June first made her pitch.

"How long do you think she'll last?" she asked.

Gai hadn't thought about it. He hadn't even imagined Jinda not being around. He had a water pump—passed down from his grandfather—that worked perfectly well after all these years. He hadn't considered his wife to be any less resilient, hadn't considered for a second she'd break down any time soon.

"Haven't thought about it," he said. "Why?"

"Well, I don't know. Don't you think it's . . . cruel?"

"Cruel?"

"Keeping her alive, I mean."

That was another thought that hadn't passed through his mind. Keeping her alive? He'd just assumed she was alive because she wanted to be. Her pulse wasn't pumping any slower. Her skin wasn't any colder. What did he have to do with that?

"No," he said.

He watched as small bubbles of tears formed in the corners of June's eyes. She turned her back to him and he heard her sniff back tears. He'd only ever seen her jolly and positive so it came as something of a surprise.

"What's wrong?"

"Nothing." She didn't turn back to him.

"Nothing? You're crying."

There was a long moment of silence during which his wife's presence in the room became obtrusive.

"You really don't know, do you, Gai?" June said. "You don't see it."

He didn't know. He didn't see. There was a lot to learn in this world of romance.

"No."

She turned back to him. Her face was a messy palette of tear drops and water trails. A face, he considered, that might benefit from a good windshield wiper.

"You don't know what I feel for you, do you?" she asked in a barely audible whisper. "You think this is all a fling and one day I'll move on and leave you."

Of course he thought that but he had the good sense to keep his mouth shut.

"Well, it isn't a fling," June's voice was breathy and damp. "I want you, Gai. I want us to spend the rest of our days together. I want to be your wife. I love you, Gai."

She scrambled to her feet with surprising agility for a big-boned woman, grabbed her body cloth from the bed, and hurried off to the washing room. Gai turned to Jinda who lay glaring at the underside of the concrete roof tiles. The ridge of dried skin saddled her shaved skull like a badly-welded diving bell.

"You hear that?" Gai asked.

That 'love' word really didn't get a lot of air-time in Paak Nam, not even amongst lovers. Once the conquest was complete, a man could pretty well put his romantic rhetoric back in the ice-chest till his next flirtation. But, coming from a fine-looking woman like June, and with all its 'rest of our days together' wrapping, that word rattled around for some time in Gai's mind. He'd never encountered the like of it. It became a kind of obsession to him. He was a simple man and it took a while for the three ingredients from June's speech to come together to make a dish he could swallow. June wanted to marry him. That couldn't happen as long as Jinda was around. He was the only one keeping his wife alive. Even though June hadn't mentioned it again, Gai returned to the subject a week later. He was eating spiced fish-paste with his fingers directly from the banana leaf. June was washing Jinda's clothes in the plastic bowl they used to scale fish.

"Were you serious?" he asked.

"About what?"

"You know . . . marrying me. Spending the rest of our days together?"

"It doesn't matter," she said, and smiled as if it really didn't. "I know you don't want to."

"I didn't say that."

"You didn't say anything. That tells me you don't."

"But, I do."

"Do what?"

"I want to be with you."

"No, it wouldn't work. You don't love me."

"Yes I do."

He had no idea where it came from. It was as if, quite out of the blue, he'd coughed up a live crab. Something in him willed the words to retreat. Perhaps she hadn't caught them. The sound of the waves on the beach might have drowned him out. But he knew he was done for when she threw her bubbly fingers around his neck and pressed her cheek against his ear.

"I'm so happy," she said. "Thank you. Thank you." And she was crying again. The deal was done. It was as if a contract had been signed on that day and, by agreeing to the main condition, he had inadvertently committed himself to all the subliminal clauses.

It wasn't until a few nights later that he realized just how serious the transaction had been. June usually slept at her cousin's house of a night to maintain an image of respectability so he was surprised when she turned up at seven with an overnight bag and a new hairstyle.

"I'm taking the night train to Bangkok," she told him.

His heart dropped into the numb interior of his gammy leg.

"Why?" he asked.

"Oh, look at you. You're afraid I won't come back. That's sweet. No need to worry. I'll only be gone for a few days. That should give you plenty of time."

"Time? For what?"

June looked across at poor Jinda who sat stiffly on her rattan chair staring at a space to the left of the kitten poster she used to love so much. There was no purpose, no hope in her eyes.

"You can't let her suffer like this, Gai."

"What are you saying?"

"You know what needs to be done. When I come back I expect it to all be over."

"I can't . . ."

"It's for her benefit even more than ours."

June took his hand and placed it on her chest. He could feel her passionate heart flap in her breast like a frenzied sprat eaten alive by a jellyfish. That electrifying memory remained even after she'd climbed behind the village motorcycle taxi-rider and sped off to the station. The buzz still crackled at the tips of his fingers as he knelt in front of Jinda. He looked for some trace of their story on her face but the page was empty. He put his hand against her breast and it was as cool and lifeless as *roti* dough. If there was truly a heart inside, it barely beat for her, and as sure as the moon rose from out of the sea, it certainly didn't beat for him. June was right. He couldn't let her suffer any more. He had to put her out of their combined misery.

He sat on the sand that night amid the bamboo and the tangled nets and the chunks of polystyrene that washed up on the beach each day. He studied the tips of the unimpressive waves and wondered how best to kill his wife. It had to appear natural. He could starve her to death and claim she'd refused to eat, but that might take a week or two and June would be back in four days. He was no genius with potions or poisons so he had no idea how to spike her rice. He could hold a pillow over her face but that was too direct, too callous. He doubted he could go through with it. By the time the sun had given the Eastern seaboard a new coat of light to help it on its day, every conceivable form of murder available to an uncomplicated man had passed through his mind. When he limped back to his house, Gai, with eyes saggy and dark, knew what he had to do.

Jinda had certain motor functions that had survived the coconut. Eating and defecating at the appropriate moments were instinctive to her, and she could walk, albeit without a sense of direction or purpose. If Gai sat her on a chair she would remain there. But if he stood her and gave her a slight prod, she would amble in a straight line until she came to an obstacle. Gai often wondered whether, in her mind, she was completing that fateful whisky-addled walk home from the funeral.

Their land—actually Jinda's family land—comprised of five acres of tall coconut trees. It extended from a small municipal access road at the front, all the way to the sea. The beach and the road were sparsely trafficked and most of the plantation was concealed behind bushy fir trees. It was unlikely that anyone saw Gai launch his wife in the direction of a tree and not run to help her when she bumped into it. Her path blocked, she stood with her nose to the bark, red ants dropping onto her shoulders from the low-hanging branches. But Gai left her standing there. He left her there for the greater part of the morning, checking every now and then to see whether a nut had dropped on her head.

This was his master plan, his brilliant conception. Jinda had a propensity for standing under coconut trees and being hit by falling nuts. Nobody would accuse or blame him if she'd wandered into a drop-zone and been finished off. Who would be surprised? Her poor husband couldn't be expected to watch her twenty-four hours a day. But, by midday, although nuts had dropped in six or seven locations, none had fallen from the tree beside his wife. He knew he couldn't merely climb up a ladder and throw a coconut onto her head. He didn't have it in him. He was a poor liar. It had to be in some respects an accident, otherwise even the most superficial questioning from officer Yanee at the Bang Maprao police box would lead to a confession. Gai escorted Jinda back to the pavilion and gave her some lunch and wiped her mouth. He then selected a tree more resplendent with overripe nuts, placed her favourite rattan chair beneath it, and sat Jinda down.

With a monsoon wind building off the gulf there was a veritable rainfall of nuts that afternoon. One even dropped from the tree that towered above Jinda, but it landed with a thump on the opposite side. Gai knew in his heart that the cluster of coconuts above his wife was eager to fall on her and decided they needed a little coaxing. The old family Toyota truck was collecting rust beside the house but it still functioned. Gai kicked it into life and drove toward the beach, being careful not to get himself stuck in the loose sand they'd used to fill the land. He lined up his tree in the rearview mirror, stepped on the gas and reversed into the trunk with a crunch. Nothing happened. Again and again he tried, but apart from smashing a tail light, the battering appeared to have no effect on the tree. Then, to his surprise, an enormous nut dropped. It came crashing into the windshield, turning it into a hailstorm of glass pellets and folding the hood into the shape of a taco before falling to the ground. Gai, bruised from the reversing and bloodied from the shattering, looked in his wing mirror to see his wife sitting unfazed on her favourite rattan chair. This accident was proving a lot harder to engineer than he'd envisaged.

Like all the local coconut planters, Gai hired monkey handlers once a month. The fiery grey-brown macaques they brought with them never failed to give the impression they had better things to do. Their resentment was clear from the way they glared at humans and scowled and bared their sharp teeth. They seemed to know the day of reckoning was at hand when coconut monkeys would inherit the earth. Then we'd see who's up a tree in a dog collar, brother. But old Pah's monkey was one of the most civil of the gang. It might have been due to the fact that Pah was blind and all the glaring and scowling in the world wouldn't leave him feeling intimidated. Blindness had come to Pah late in life and the plantation owners who had used his service when he was sighted felt obliged to keep him in work. All old Pah had to do was hold onto the rope and ask the owners to lead them to the trees they wanted harvested. There were no complaints.

The animal's good nature might also have been due to the fact that she was female. It was virtually unheard of for coconut collectors to recruit a female macaque. They were generally moody and unreliable. But old Pah didn't seem to have any trouble with her. He called his animal Solo because she worked alone, knew which trees to climb and which nuts to release. As a diversion on this second day of attempted murder, Gai took Pah and Solo to four other trees before arriving at the towering monster beneath which sat his wife looking aimlessly in the direction of the ocean.

Pah called for his monkey to climb but Solo stalled at the tree's base and made a threatening charge towards Jinda. When the immobile lady failed to react, Solo shrugged and scratched her head and proceeded up the slender trunk. Once nestled amongst the branches that umbrella'd the clusters of ripe nuts, she seemed more in her element. Looking down on the world of lesser creatures. Looking down on Jinda in her favourite rattan chair. To Gai's paranoid mind, the monkey seemed to be aware of the silent woman, sensing her vulnerability. So, when she felt her rope jerk and heard the "Pull!" instruction from her owner, Solo began her work at the far side of the tree.

Some monkeys were biters and chewed through the stems. Others twisted the nuts loose with their hands. Solo liked to hold onto something stable and twirl the nuts with her feet like a circus performer. On this day, the coconuts were mature and easily separated from their bunches. Five, six, seven nuts dropped to the ground far from Jinda.

"Pull," said Pah, and Solo dispatched several more nuts that rained to the left and right of the woman seated below. There was a large bunch directly above Jinda but Solo gave it only a cursory glance before starting her way back down. In her mind, her work was complete.

"Is she done?" asked Pah.

"Not even nearly," Gai told him. "There's a complete cluster she hasn't touched."

Old Pah yanked at the rope. "Up," he shouted.

Solo checked her descent. She was two meters down the trunk. She looked earthward at the woman and then skyward at the nuts. As if rent in two, she bared her teeth and let out a troubled cry.

"She's been getting grumpy of late," old Pah told Gai. "Must be menopause. My wife had it bad. She stopped cooking and spent her days swinging on the hammock." He turned his milky eyes to the sky. "Up!" he yelled.

Gai watched the monkey climb back up to the final bunch. The wily animal was obviously troubled. She bounced and beat her chest and kicked up a stink until Gai was certain she'd baulk at her task. But, amidst all the head-shaking and screeching and teeth-baring, a decision had to be made, get fed tonight . . . or not. And morals obviously took a back seat to food because Solo held onto a frond with her left hand and used her feet and her right hand to twist loose the largest nut of the bunch.

With not an ounce of dramatic ability or conviction, Gai suddenly called out, "Jinda. What are you doing out here? Get back to the house. Look out!"

June arrived on the 6 a.m. train from Bangkok. She dropped off her things at her cousin's, had a nap, attended to a little business downtown, and then took a taxi motorcycle to Gai's house. Her future beau was sitting in the bamboo pavilion smoking a hand-rolled cigarette. She'd never seen him smoke before.

"Gai?"

He waved half-heartedly as she climbed from the bike and walked down the slope from the road. She was carry-ing a large cardboard box tied with blue nylon string.

"I bought you a few things from the big city," she said, looking beyond Gai towards the house. "Is she ...?"

She noticed Gai's fingers shake when he pulled the cigarette from his mouth to speak.

"I think she's gone," he said.

"You think?"

"It's a long story. Yai from administration at the Lang Suan hospital just came by ten minutes ago. He said they want me over there, urgent. It wasn't looking good, he said."

"Jinda's there?"

"She got hit by a coconut the day before yesterday. She's been in a coma ever since. She's on ... what do you call it? Life support? It's been touch and go."

June couldn't hide her smile. "She got hit by a coconut?"

"Old Pah's monkey was working the trees."

She squeezed his hand. "You're a lot cleverer than you look, Mr. Gai. A blind witness and a guilty monkey. I don't know how you did it but it's brilliant. I mean, it's great for her too."

"I don't feel so wonderful."

"You'll get over it. And just think about the land."

"The land?"

"Oh, Gai. You're so ... I don't know what the word is. With Jinda gone the land becomes yours."

"No, it belongs to her family."

"And they're all gone too. She was the last of the line down here."

"There's a niece. She's in the north somewhere."

"Maybe so. But she's been out of the picture for too long. She probably doesn't even know she's got relatives in the south. All you have to do is post a notice with the public prosecutor's office telling them you're the new executor, and, if nobody claims Jinda's land inside of a month, it's all yours."

"Are you sure about that?"

"I was at the council offices this morning."

"You were?"

"Just visiting a friend, you know? I asked in passing."

"I didn't think about land or inheritance or anything like that."

"I know you didn't, sweetheart. That's why I'm so fond of you. And that's why you need me to look after you. You know they just sold a plot of beachfront land down the coast to some foreigners for five million baht? Five million, and it's half the size of yours."

Gai laughed without humour.

"This has been coconut land going back eight generations. Jinda wouldn't ever think about selling it."

"Jinda won't be thinking about a lot of things from now on, will she? It's just you and me now." She squeezed the inside of his thigh and let her hand linger there. "And you can do whatever you like."

The Toyota was a wreck, so Gai hitched a ride to the market at Paak Nam and took the truck-bus into Lang Suan. As he bounced on the wooden bench, a lot of conflicting thoughts rattled around inside him. The amount "five million" figured prominently, as did the public prosecutor and the thought that he could do anything he liked. He wondered why June should suddenly show an interest in land. She'd never mentioned it before. He'd just told her his wife was probably dead and she launched into a discussion on real estate. But perhaps different people handled grief in different ways. Since the second coconut split Jinda's head north to south, leaving her looking like a Phillips roundhead screw, he'd found himself crying a lot. There must have been a lifetime of tears locked inside him because he'd sat on the beach all through that first night and bawled his eyes out. It was a wonder his parched old body could ever contain that much water. The reservoir hadn't run dry till the morning June came back from Bangkok.

When he told the two white-uniformed nurses at reception who he was and who he'd come to see, they exchanged a glance that suggested each had been expecting the other to act calm. Instead, they both panicked. One even dropped the phone before she could call her supervisor. Gai interpreted this as embarrassment. Nobody wanted to be the one to tell him his wife was dead. He tried to make it more comfortable for them.

"She's gone, isn't she?" he said, somewhere between a question and a statement. But still nobody was prepared to give him a definite 'yes' until the hospital manager came out to reception. He led Gai firmly by the arm into his office.

"Yes," said the smooth-faced man, wiping his glasses on a wad of gauze. "She died this morning." Death was obviously a difficult subject for hospital workers. They all seemed to be taking it badly. Perhaps it was a failure that nobody was prepared to take the blame for.

"That's all right," said Gai. He meant that he was relieving the hospital of its guilt, but it came out sounding as if it was all right for Jinda to be dead. He didn't know how to fix the misconception. The administrator stared briefly at the older man then told him he needed to find a paper for the bereaved to sign. He stood, nodded, and left Gai alone in the simple concrete office. The only window opened onto a mimosa bush whose scent carried traces of disinfectant. A green bean-eater bird sat on a low branch opening and closing its beak but no sound came from it. Gai wondered whether it was a mute.

It must have been twenty minutes before the office door opened again and Gai was surprised to see, not the administrator, but his old friend Yanee of the Bang Maprao police box. The policeman smiled and walked into the room followed by a more senior officer Gai didn't recognize.

"Afternoon, Gai," Yanee said. He sat at the desk and the other man leaned against the wall beside the window. The bird fled.

"Hello, Yanee," said Gai. He nodded at the other man but there was no reaction.

"The mind's a funny thing," Yanee said, as if they were midway through a conversation.

"I'm sure you're right."

"Take Jinda, for example."

And, at that moment, Gai knew it was all over. He knew instinctively he'd been found out. All that remained was for him to learn why.

"What happened, Yanee?"

"Well, it's a bit like a mechanical harvester, Gai. You know sometimes those things just stop for no apparent reason. They get something stuck in their oily brains and they're dead. And the best mechanical engineer couldn't work out what's gone wrong. But all you need is to give it a thwack with a wrench and it starts up again as right as rain. No logical explanation for it. You know what I mean?"

"Yeah, I've seen that happen," Gai smiled. "Damn things."

"So, as it turns out, for the past five years, Jinda couldn't see a thing, but she could hear everything that was going on around her. Sad thing was, she couldn't tell anyone. She didn't have any way to communicate, you see? I can't begin to imagine what torture it was for her. Then, out of the blue, she gets hit on the head again and it's like that wrench. It just bangs her back to life, clicks her brain back into gear. She came round late last night, Gai, and started babbling on to the night nurse. The nurse called the duty doctor and, this morning, they called us."

"She told you about June and me?"

"And your plot to do away with her. Yeah. She told us all about that. But she seemed more disappointed in you, Gai. She said she couldn't understand how you could be so stupid. How you could think that girl was interested in you when there was all that prime real estate up for grabs. Your wife didn't care that you found yourself a little recreation. She didn't begrudge you that. But she really had a desire to knock some sense into you before she went."

"Why didn't you call me in this morning?"

"Cause we didn't have a case this morning. It looked like Jinda might pull through. But she got a clot in her brain and she was gone. Then it was murder, you see, Gai? As it stands, there's still nothing settled. It's your word against hers. You could argue that she didn't know what she was saying. You could claim she was ..."

"No, Yanee. It's all true. I deserve whatever's coming to me."

"I thought you'd see it like that."

"But ..."

"What?"

"I do wish you'd called me. I wish I could have been around when she was talking. There was a lot I wanted to say. I've missed her, Yanee. I've missed her really bad since that day."

"She was a good woman, Gai."

"Yes, she was a good woman. I didn't appreciate her. But, it wasn't just that." He stood and walked to the door. The senior officer took him by the wrist and put handcuffs on him. There was no struggle. "I loved her, Yanee," he said.

The two policemen exchanged a glance. Old Gai's mind had definitely gone.

"Of course you did, Gai. Of course you did."

Coconuts

Our friend Jimm's father has a permanent lump on his head the size of a cricket ball. It's a reminder of the day he was hit on the head by a coconut and wandered around for three days wondering where he lived. Unless you pull up a chair and sit directly beneath a bunch of ripe coconuts for a week or two, the odds against being hit by one are quite phenomenal. You'd have to think heaven had something against you. There's statistically more chance of a buffalo hijacking your Honda.

So, using a falling coconut as a murder device seemed like a fitting metaphor for the pace of life here on the coast. I wanted to paint a picture of the environment and the characters as a contrast to the Thailand you've seen in Ode to a Siam Square Pizza. Same country – different planet.

With the begrudging knowledge of their wives, and the almost nonchalant blessing of friends and other relatives, two of our neighbours are supporting mistresses. It seems endemic in Thai society. I mentioned to Jess, as we were trying to fit in down here, perhaps I should find myself a little filly on the side. (The stitches come out on Wednesday. The doctor said the scar will be very faint)

Better that than the alternative. There are numerous stories of wayward husbands waking from a drunken slumber to find they've been relieved of a few ounces of valuable meat.

Forked

THE PIANO TUNER ran through ascending chords, enjoying the resistance of the heavy ivory keys. His balding head was bent forward, his eyes closed as he listened. The notes rose to the darkened ceiling of the recital hall near Warsaw's Old Market Square, then dissipated like smoke, the last notes he would ever play and no record of them apart from a distant hum in his memory. He closed the lid and wiped away his tears with a large white handkerchief. The piano was pitch perfect. Only he was out of tune now.

On the flight home he used the headphones as a barrier between him and the gum augmentation specialist beside him. He refused refreshments, closed his eyes and considered what he could expect at Heathrow. He decided it would be informal—conservatively British. Not, he imagined, a wail of sirens or a flash of black flak jackets passing in front of his eyes like a bump on the head. Rather, a nod from the turbaned immigration officer and the approach of a tall young man with a neck bearing wounds from a cheap razor. Beside him a dark-skinned female in a black suit—the younger sister of a Jamaican undertaker, perhaps. A slight self-consciously polite nod from the young man and the words, "Thomas Cedric Cooksley?"

Thomas would not render them unconscious with a series of strategically-placed blows nor sprint back into the labyrinth of tunnels. He would not commandeer a baggage tractor and flee across a busy runway. The police were there at his invitation so he would nod and smile politely, perhaps ask them if they were well.

"You are under arrest for the murder of Mrs. Evangaline Victoria Cooksley."

This would be followed by a brief caution, an unobtrusive hand around the arm, and an escorted stroll to a waiting police car. In England, such matters were dealt with in a far more civilized fashion than across the Atlantic.

Not wanting to leave matters in the hands of an incompetent investigator, when he'd phoned the Metropolitan Police emergency line three days earlier and made his confession, he had provided them with the date and time of his arrival from Europe. He hadn't given them the flight number because he preferred to be arrested nicely on his home soil, not bundled into a Polish police car, beaten senseless and manhandled home by neckless goons. He requested just one last period of dignity before joining the ranks of the criminal class.

In case they thought his call was a hoax, he'd given them his home address, 32 Ridley Road, Hammersmith, West London, and told them it wouldn't be necessary to break down the door because there was a key under the front doormat. He knew the police would be dismayed at the thought, but he explained that it was sewn into a small pocket on the underside of the mat. The only danger was that somebody might steal the mat itself.

He explained that they would find his wife on the floor of their bedroom in front of his mother-in-law's oak dressing table. She could be identified by the pale blue house coat with small dark blue Chinese dragons on the lapels and a tuning fork embedded in her left eye. The fork was premium nickel-plated with an uncustomary long handle.

He'd given that fork a good deal of thought over the past three days and nights. He'd wondered, given its peculiar shape, exactly how he'd been able to kill her with it. Firstly, it must have taken tremendous force to be able to pierce her eye. How was a man as meek as he able to summon such power? That was a question he imagined his solicitor might ask the court at his trial. But there had to be no more doubt of his abilities. The only way he might avoid this question would be to do without a lawyer and represent himself. He could then choose not to ask himself such questions. But the British legal system strongly discouraged self-representation so he'd need a strong rebuttal. It would be this, that forty years of living with a woman who constantly reminded him of his one major failing can well up in a man, however timid. He'd been driven to distraction by hearing again and again how badly she'd married. She'd believed her fiancé would become a well-known concert pianist but look what she'd ended up with, a piano tuner.

"You had the acumen," she would remind him. "You had the technical ability. It's unthinkable that you were unable to make a name for yourself on the international circuit. Pathetic!"

Of course it was thinkable because it had happened. A number of young men and women every bit as talented as him had graduated from The Royal Academy. Yes, for acumen and technical skills he was in the top five percent. But modern music had sought to compete for fans with the other musical genres. It wasn't pianos people came to look at, it was the impresarios who tamed the beasts—the personalities, the eccentricities, the sex. The piano was no longer an instrument; it was a dance partner, a lover. If a pianist could do no more than sit for three hours, dead from the wrists upward, modern audiences would elect to stay home and spend their money on a decent music system. Sadly, Thomas Cooksley had no personality of which the piano might become an extension. His music was vibrant but he himself was dull. His piano had multiple orgasms while he snoozed at the keyboard.

And, over those forty years, barely a day went by when she didn't remind him in one way or another.

"Cornflakes? We could be eating fresh muesli on a balcony overlooking Lake d'Orta if you'd just fulfilled your potential."

Yes, that was where the force came from. That, to the utter surprise of the Crown Prosecution, is what he'd own up to. No inadequacies in Thomas Cooksley.

"The hate built over forty years till one day it exploded in me."

But, surprised as he was that he had the strength to bury a tuning fork into his wife's eye, he was even more surprised that it could kill her. He was looking forward to hearing the coroner's report at the trial. There had been remarkably little blood. He had two theories of his own. His first was that the fork had punctured her brain. The C pitch had reverberated through her cranium and tuned her senseless. The second, and more likely scenario, was that she had turned to the mirror, seen a tuning fork protruding from her eye, and had a heart attack. Her heart was no stronger than her fidelity. Either way she was just as dead.

If he were to be honest, he'd been more concerned about the cat than his wife. He'd arrived at Heathrow to catch his flight, called the Metropolitan Police to confess, and was sitting in the departure lounge reading the *Daily Express* when he remembered Ginger. Their cat of many years was almost entirely confined to the house and a small patch of garden around the back door. His fence-climbing days were far behind him. Thomas doubted the police would open a can of Whiskas chopped liver and wait around long enough for him to relieve himself of it. But Ginger was a good-mannered beast and he would have allowed himself to blow up rather than defecate in the house.

So Thomas had called the senior partner of his two-man piano tuning company, Alistair McWiggen, the grand old queen of Queen Anne Grands.

"Wiggy," he'd said. "It's me."

"Ye Gods. You've missed your flight. Heaven help us. The Warsaw Symphony and we've let them down." He made a fainting sound with his breath.

It was unthinkable that Thomas might miss an appointment or let down the firm.

"Don't get into a flap, old girl. I'm at the airport. It's just there's been a little to-do at my house."

To the accompaniment of squeals and shrieks, he'd explained his predicament. By the time he got around to asking the big soft fairy if he'd be so kind as to look after his cat, the senior partner was aflood with tears. It was uncertain whether the message had been received, but by then they had announced Thomas's flight for the third time. Warsaw beckoned. Ginger was entrusted to fate. The airplane's meandering taxi journey around the Heathrow tarmac took almost as long as the flight itself. When finally they found a vacant gate, Thomas was surprised at how unwobbly his legs were, how confident his stride. He joined the passport queue and scanned the far side of the booths for the tall white and short black. He handed his passport to the unsmiling

Sikh and was surprised that the picture therein still bore a passing resemblance to the murderer at the front of the immigration line.

"Welcome home, Mr. Cooksley," the bearded man said and handed back the passport. It wasn't a greeting, merely one of a list of 'phrases to make our officers seem like they care', plucked from the manual. To Thomas it sounded like a bluff. Until he was moved along by security, he stood awaiting his arrest in the area clearly marked 'no waiting'. He allowed his mind to trip over possibilities. Perhaps the Met hadn't believed him, hadn't bothered to visit his house. Perhaps they had the wrong date or had become tired of waiting. Perhaps, heaven forbid, Eva wasn't dead. She'd answered the doorbell with a towel over her head pretending to be fresh from the shower. No, no, she'd had no pulse. She hadn't so much as flinched when he kicked her. He was certain she'd be smelling to high heaven by now. What if the cat had eaten parts of her then exploded all over the new bedroom wallpaper? The possibilities were too awful to consider.

The uncertainty, the unexpected, these were what set off a tremor in Thomas's old legs and a flutter in his stomach. He could tolerate the suspense for no longer than was absolutely necessary. He ignored the UNDERGROUND sign and went straight to the taxi stand out front. The rates were exorbitant and there probably wouldn't be much change from the Warsaw cheque, but he had to get home as soon as possible. The East African driver was in no more of a mood for conversation than his passenger. He noted the address and dedicated himself to his task. It was the type of February day when the dirty clouds squatted low over the streets and suffocated the buildings. It was like driving through a carwash in a grey cave. The driver swore in Kiswahili every time a truck kicked up filthy water onto his windows.

Thomas imagined a dark novel in which the protagonist was off to confront a situation worse than death. No writer could have painted a more dour journey than West London at four-thirty on a drizzly Wednesday. Every dripping person they passed had a shadow of doom tattooed on his face. Each oncoming headlight flashed a warning of the dread it was escaping. After an hour they came off the A4 and began to angle through the gloomy suburbs whose lights seemed low on batteries. A country that dispensed daylight so sparingly could surely invest in streetlights that offered more than a duckpond of light every twenty yards.

Thirty-two Ridley Road feigned innocence from the outside. It stood solid and bleak, unable to breathe through the rain that beat against its façade. Its glass was black. Its brick was pitted with neglect. As the taxi pulled away, Thomas stood on the pavement letting the cold rain soak into his woolen suit—his raincoat over his arm. His wheeled case stood beside him like a black retriever awaiting its master's signal to go forward.

The key was in its pocket under the doormat and when he turned the metal in the lock it sounded to him like a dentist removing a tooth with pliers. He let the door swing open but remained on the step. He looked into the darkness and, without question, the darkness looked back at him. He flicked on the passage light and took in a deep breath. All he could smell was *pot pourri*. According to the television, the stench of a body three days into its decay should be vile enough to peel paint. Either Evangeline's body was no longer in the house, or Evangeline was not dead.

With the front door wide open behind him, the uninvited rain rudely blowing through it, he walked to the staircase and turned the dimmer control for the upstairs landing. From the bottom step he could see the top of the master bedroom door. Something was out of place, odd, downstairs but his mind was racing, already on the landing. As he climbed the creaky staircase more and more of the bedroom came into view until he was standing in front of it. He sniffed again. Nothing. The bedroom light switch was a yard inside the door and in order to reach it he had to take a step into the shadow. He was fumbling across the wallpaper when he heard the voice from the bed.

"Hello, Thomas. I've been waiting for you."

Thomas stumbled back against the frame of the door. His legs gave up on him completely and he slid down onto the blue shag carpeting. He could barely make out a shadow on the high mattress. It reached for the bedside lamp and clicked the button. The piano tuner's mouth fell open with the weight of a hangman's trap door. His damp eyes took in the pale blue housecoat with dragon lapels, incongruous fluffy pink slippers, long brown hair. Had it occurred to Thomas to breathe at all during his journey to the upper floor, he might not have passed out. As he'd never fainted before, and believed it to be a condition reserved exclusively for frail and easily shocked women, he assumed he was dying.

It was impossible to tell how long Thomas had been unconscious. His partner, Alistair, stood to one side of the bed wringing a flannel into a small plastic bowl. As always, he was impeccably dressed in a tweed waistcoat and bow tie. He opened up the cloth and placed it above Thomas's eyebrows. As the forehead extended all the way to the back, there had been no need to fold it. It felt painfully ice cold and sent a shudder down the junior partner's spine.

"Did you see her?" Thomas asked.

"Oh, I certainly did, my sweets."

"I thought she was dead. I was certain . . ."

"And you were totally spot on to believe so, Thomas."

"But . . . ?"

"Look, I'm such a Wally-wanker, I admit it. I was waiting for you to get back. Couldn't resist trying on some of Eva's things one last time. I dropped off. Perhaps you could find it in your heart to forgive me?"

Thomas sat up.

"Why haven't I been arrested? Didn't the police come to find Anj?"

"They did, darling. They did."

"And?"

"And they met her."

"Wiggy, you're giving me a worse headache than I deserve."

"You called me from the airport. You told me you'd confessed to the police."

"Yes?"

"And I got here before them. Justice moves slowly in Grande Bretagne. I almost gave myself a hernia putting her body in your old W.H. Paling Upright downstairs."

"You put her in the piano? But you said they'd met her."

"Well, technically. You see, Evangeline and I are the same size. And she does have . . . or, I suppose I have to say, did have a splendid range of rather expensive cosmetics."

"You passed yourself off as Anj? Wiggy, how could you?"

"Why not? Anj didn't look like Anj without her face on. I was more than a passing resemblance to your dead wife."

"They believed you were a woman?"

"Absolutely, darling."

"McWiggen?"

"All right, perhaps not entirely sucked in. But they did believe we had 'a relationship' at some level. The modern bobby is rather more broadminded than we give him credit for. They asked to have a look around. They saw all our holiday snaps and our bedroom, minus one soiled Afghan rug. I told them about our little fight and how you like to get your bitchy revenge on me. I cried a little and talked them out of pressing charges against you for filing a falsie. And they left. Rather dashing young sergeant. I almost cracked a feel as he was leaving but that would have been pushing the dildo a touch, don't you think?"

"Where's Anj?"

"I nailed down the lid of your piano and had Alan and Bertrand come by to pick it up and take it to the workshop. That night I gave myself another hernia hauling the slovenly bitch out and into the truck. I took her for a ride to the new concert hall they're building at Burgh Heath. The cement in one of the pillar foundations was just damp enough. I could probably have found somewhere closer to bury her but, given her desire to be on the concert circuit, I thought it was charmingly fitting. Don't you?"

"Wiggy, I thought you liked her."

"Loathed her, sweetheart. Loathed her. I detested the way she put you down all the time. But she was your wife and it wasn't my place. I've been saying a little prayer beside my bed all these years that you'd take an axe to her."

"You did all this for me?"

"Isn't it brilliant, the things a man would do for love?"

Forked!

To my great surprise, I won a short story competition with this one. I'd never won a short story competition before. In fact I'd never entered one. That's a one-hundred percent average. With results like that, a boy might be tempted to develop a false sense of his own brilliance. I was so inspired, I put together this collection.

I'd joined the International Thriller Writers Association a few years earlier (more because I was international than I was thrilling) and they invited entries — the winner to have his or her story recorded on their Chopin Manuscript audio book. The first line of the short was taken from the first line of the book. Competitors merely had to provide the next 800 or so. I love that kind of thing. It makes for a fun diversion.

I'd only ever written one short story before ("Has Anyone Seen Mrs. Lightswitch?" *Damn Near Dead*, Busted Flush Press — also included in this collection). But every now and then you stumble across something you have a knack for — like gutting fish or beheading coconuts with a machete. You know somewhere in the gene pool, Uncle Oof was slicing coconuts and writing short stories on the cave wall.

I needed an analogy for short story writing. It was already clear to me that writing a novel is labour. It's house building. You have to work on it a brick at a time with the floor plan up on the wall. Every now and then you have to tear something down to make it fit. Sometimes the plumber comes and tells you the toilet's on the wrong side of the bathroom (you can tell we're in the middle of building, can't you?)

A short story is more of a shed. It goes up overnight, doesn't have to match anything, and if you don't like the look of it you just tear it down and make rabbit hutches. OK, so perhaps analogies aren't my strong point.

ABOUT THE AUTHOR

Colin Cotterill was born in London in 1952. He trained as a Physical Education teacher and set off on a world tour that didn't ever come to an end. He worked as a Physical Education instructor in Israel, a primary school teacher in Australia, a big brother for educationally disadvantaged adults in the United States, and a university lecturer in Japan, before spending the greater part of his latter years in Southeast Asia.

In Thailand where he has lived off and on since 1985 Colin has worked as a teacher, newspaper and magazine columnist, TV language program writer and producer, and NGO worker. He spent four years in Laos, initially with UNESCO.

Eight years ago, Colin became involved in child protection. He established an NGO in the south of Thailand and later joined ECPAT, an international organization that combats child prostitution and pornography. He set up their training programme for caregivers.

All the while, Colin continued with his two other passions, cartooning and writing. He has so far written more than ten books—seven of them crime novels in the Dr. Siri Paiboun series set in Laos, which have been nominated for and won several awards including the CWA Dagger in the Library in 2009.

At present Colin writes (and draws) full-time. He lives in Chumphon on the Gulf of Siam with his wife, Jess, and a pack of unruly dogs. He listens to jazz, rides his bicycle to the post office, and isn't averse to the odd glass of red.

Lightning Source UK Ltd.
Milton Keynes UK
12 July 2010
156900UK00007B/8/P